BOOK OF SMILES

Lorraine Beard

ISBN: 978-1-4710-6607-8

First Published 2021 by
Lorraine Beard

Printed by LuLu.com for Lorraine Beard

There's no age limit on fun!

Table of Contents

Foreword	1
Introduction	3
1	1
2	4
3	6
4	11
5	15
6	20
7	22
8	26
9	30
10	36
11	40
12	44
13	46
14	50
15	52
16	54
17	56
18	60
19	63
20	66
21	69
22	72
23	73
24	75
25	79
26	83
27	85
28	90
29	92
30	97
31	100
32	104
33	106
34	109
35	114
36	119
37	121
38	125
39	127
40	133
Conclusion	136

Foreword

Some time around 2010, I was doing a weekly Internet radio show, living out my dream of being a radio broadcaster, minus the overrated inconvenience of getting paid for it. I started chatting with one of my listeners, someone named Alex. As we chatted on Twitter, I wondered—quite reasonably, I thought—Who is this guy Alex, anyway? Soon Alex, my then-girlfriend Caroline, and I started voice-chatting on Skype, and I figured out very quickly that Alex wasn't "this guy" at all.

After a few of these chats, Alex asked us if it was okay for her to bring her friend Lou into the conversations as well. Naturally, I wondered—quite reasonably, I thought—Who is this guy Lou, anyway? I soon figured out that Lou wasn't "this guy" either. Having straightened out these identity issues, the four of us have gone on to develop a very close friendship indeed.

When Lou came to visit my now-wife Caroline and me in 2019, and for an all-too-brief stay in 2020, I quickly learned that she's as much of a joy to be around in person as she is to talk to at a distance. We quickly got into a routine, which I came to treasure deeply. The way it worked was this: Lou slept in our living room —the budgies didn't mind. Lou would get up first and do whatever she did in the morning. I'd come out into the living room some time later, where I worked from home, and Caroline came out some time after that. While I was preparing to work, Lou and I would have these incredible conversations: completely unscripted, wonderful conversations about anything and everything. We bounced ideas off of each other, told each other stories about our lives (many of which you'll read here), laughed, and cried, as very good friends do. I can't wait for her next visit, so the tradition can continue.

Lou is an incredible person, always willing to see the bright side, the funny side, to find reasons to laugh where one might not normally see what you're going to find in the pages of this book. Lou can also make you think, and look at yourself a little differently. Maybe the things that frustrate you aren't as frustrating as they seem; maybe if you stop and think about it, that annoying mishap that seems determined to ruin your day can be turned around and smiled about instead. In sharing these anecdotes, Lou uses her own experiences and her reactions to them to help us all shed light on our own experiences, and react better to them.

You won't learn all there is to learn about Lou in this book. It's not what she's trying to do, which is a good thing because there's way more to her than you'll read here. But what you will learn is part of why I, why Caroline, and why so many others of us, consider this amazing woman of God to be one of our closest friends in the whole world.

Bruce Toews

Winnipeg, Manitoba

26 September (or as we call it, September 26), 2021

Introduction

This year, 2021, will be the year of my fortieth birthday. There are many things in life for which I'm thankful, but there are also things in life I thought I would have by now. Therefore, I have to admit that being forty wasn't something I was finding particularly easy to think about.

Thanks to some lovely friends, who seemed to enjoy reading my Facebook posts about funny things that have happened to me, I was inspired to turn something I'm not looking forward to into something which will, hopefully, bless others. I truly believe that, as it says in Proverbs, "A joyful heart is good medicine," and especially over the last year or so, we've needed that blessing of joyful laughter even more.

If you took me to a comedy evening, I'd likely not find much of it funny. I suppose you could say that I find things funny which were never actually intended to be humorous. The problem I also have is that, once I start laughing, I find it difficult to stop!

As an example, my friend Ruth and I used to sit next to one another in choir. One day, Ruth started laughing. Laughter is infectious, so I, too, started laughing. Ruth got away with it, but when I was asked why I was laughing, I had to honestly admit that I didn't know! This didn't go down very well, but I managed to hide my laughter when we were supposed to be practicing from then on—most of the time, anyway!

I really don't want this book to come across as all about me. I often laugh at myself, though, and the silly things I do, so although most of the things in this book are about me, there are situations which include others as well. Wherever possible, I've obtained the permission of those I've included.

As with many things, once you have the original idea you wonder whether you should do it or not. I was discussing the idea for the book with my closest friend, Alex, at the end of last year. We were talking about all sorts of things I could include, but I still wasn't convinced. I was cooking at the time, and it was through this that I had the confirmation that this book needed to be written.

The previous day, my dad had given me a bag of brown sugar. He'd opened it and used a small amount, but it wasn't the kind he wanted, so he put a peg on it and gave it to me, as he knew I'd use it for some sort of baking and he was probably hoping for cake. My baking cupboard was extremely full, so I had to balance it somewhere silly. I went into that cupboard while Alex and I were chatting, and out bounced the brown sugar...straight into the sink, which was full of washing up water. I quickly grabbed the bag, and was pleased to see that it was still upright. The level of the water hadn't reached the pegged part at the top, so I was relieved. It was a plastic package, so I dried it off and stood it on the side to check properly later.

The problem was, I kept finding bits of brown sugar on my hands and up my arms. I had no idea where it was coming from, and it was driving me crazy! I kept wiping down the worktops, but I still kept finding grains of sugar. I'm always washing my hands when I'm cooking, and I eventually realised I'd somehow got brown sugar on the towel I was drying my hands on. Water must have got into the package, so I couldn't save it after all. I decided there and then that I had to write this book, so here it is.

Some incidents are stand-alone, while other sections contain several incidents on a similar theme. The book is only vaguely chronological, but not completely because of how I grouped some of the stories.

I really hope the hilarity of my life gives you a smile, that's the intention anyway! I'm hoping the things which are funny to me are equally amusing to you.

As I mentioned, some of my friends have directly or indirectly encouraged me to write this book. I'd like to thank everyone who has encouraged me, but I'd particularly like to thank Lil Goertzen, Miriam Corringham, and Heather Andrews. I'd also like to thank Alex Banwell for reading things to see if they make sense, and putting up with my bouncing ideas about. A huge thank-you also goes out to Colin Owen, for designing the cover and inputting everything into the templates to get the book on kindle and in print. Finally, I'd like to thank my good friend Bruce Toews for proofreading this book. My grammar and typing can be hilarious at times, especially when I start writing in the same way I talk!

1

It's funny the things we remember. Some people can't remember very far back in their childhood, but I have a few very clear memories. I think I may have been just two years old when I discovered a new place in our garden.

I spent a lot of time playing outside, dolls and dolls' prams, a three-wheeler bike with a tipper on the back, and a little blue car kept me entertained for hours. At the front of the house was a concrete area and around the side was another patio. To get from one to the other, there were three steps to go down. There were several sets of steps around our house, and although I could go up and down most of them as I wished, I knew that I wasn't allowed to go down the steps to the cellar on my own. I wasn't too tempted anyway, as I got to go down there often with Mum or Dad.

There was quite a bit of metal fencing around the patios, galvanised steel fencing with lots of tall poles lined up, with interesting swirly bits above them. I was following the fence along when I found the new bit of garden. I think my aim was to go down to the cellar, where I could hear Mum and Dad talking. I followed the fence and got to the open gate. There was no hand rail on the cellar steps, so I kept hold of the fence, following it closely as I made my way towards their voices. I was amazed to find There were no steps! I wondered why I'd never found this bit of garden before.

I followed that fence all the way along, until I came to a wall. I wondered how to get to the cellar from here, as Mum and Dad seemed very close to me now. I hung on tightly to the fence and stretched my leg out to see if there was a step—after all, this was a new bit of garden and perhaps I hadn't seen it before because it was dangerous. There was a step, but I couldn't reach down it. I was disappointed as I pulled myself back up and shouted to my parents.

They hurried out of the cellar, and I don't know exactly what they said, apart from telling me not to move. One stood far below me, while the other ran up the steps and around the fence, and lifted me over it.

It seemed I hadn't found a new bit of garden at all. I'd walked along the four inch ledge on the inside of the fence, with the flight of steps leading down to the cellar right below me. By the time I'd reached the wall of the house, I was about eight feet up in the air!

***

I was a very adventurous child! I didn't seem to understand that, since I was only small, there were certain things I shouldn't attempt. One sunny afternoon when I was about two years old—I actually remember this clearly—my dad was doing something up on the roof. The ladder stretching up from the patio seemed intriguing, and I wanted to know what a roof looked like!

I must have known that I shouldn't be going up there, as I quietly abandoned the dolls I was playing with and made my way to that great temptation known as the ladder.

I'd been up ladders before. I'd wanted to know what the attic looked like, so I'd been up there with my dad. I knew how to climb ladders; so, ever so quietly, I began my ascent. It was a long way up there. I could see the window on the ground floor shining as I passed it, then came Mum and Dad's bedroom window. I knew I was really high up and nearing my destination!

Then a most disappointing thing happened. I put my hand on my dad's foot. I quite calmly announced, "Dad, I want to go on the roof."

I think there was an exclamation of "Dearo!" or something very similar. I was told to stay there and not move, before he called my mum. I tried to reason that if he went on up onto the roof, I could get up there too, but he wasn't having any of it and my chance was gone.

Disappointment filled me as Mum climbed the ladder behind me, then made me climb back down with her holding onto me. I remember feeling a bit confused about all the fuss. After all, I'd climbed up there by myself and I didn't see why I needed her to hang on to me on the way down.

I never did get to see the roof of the house. For some strange reason, there were never ladders around for me to climb after that. I wonder why!!!

I did get to climb on the porch roof with my dad's help when I was about ten; there was also the roof of my playhouse which Dad had built. That, at least, was a sloping roof, but not half as fun as the roof of the house, as it wasn't very high. My dad was happy to teach me to climb trees, so I made the most of that.

My cousin Martyn is about four and a half years younger than me. Of my cousins who lived nearby when I was growing up, Martyn and I were the closest in age. We spent a lot of time together and had all sorts of adventures.

I think the first memorable adventure took place when Martyn was about two years old. We were playing on the steps at the front of my house, when Martyn seemed to stop moving and said he was stuck. I went to see what had happened and found he had put his head between the vertical bars of the metal fencing. I could see I wasn't able to help, as he did seem to be well and truly stuck. I ran into the house shouting, "Mum! Mum! Martyn's got his head stuck in the fence."

I don't know what Mum expected, but she came straight out. He was indeed stuck. He couldn't get his head back through, as his ears were stopping him. So, Mum picked him up and turned him upside down. His head came through and he was free. Thankfully he never tried that again.

***

A year or so later we were playing on the same steps. They used to lead up to a gate, which led onto a public footpath. That gate wasn't used anymore, so it had been blocked off.

When you got to the top of the steps, you had a perfect, or maybe not so perfect, view of the neighbour's garden. Unfortunately, this garden was full of all sorts of rubbish. Lawn mowers, car tires, you name it, it was probably there.

So, when the neighbour walked down the path towards his house, three-year-old Martyn called loudly to him, in a very strong forest accent, "Oy you, you've got a load of junk 'an't you?"

I never heard the response, as I grabbed Martyn by the arm and dragged him down the steps and into the house. When I told Mum what had happened, Martyn insisted, "Well he has!" We couldn't argue with that, but I don't think I played on the steps again for a while.

3

I was always an adventurous child! I was afraid of nothing, apart from thunder, fires, and ceilings falling down!

My first bike was a little three-wheeler with a tipper on the back. I usually had it full of dolls, unless Dad was building something; then it was full of gravel and I was supposedly "helping"! I got my first two-wheeled bike for my fourth birthday, but it had an unusual name before I even had it. Let's just say I was in the car with Mum and Dad when Dad said something he shouldn't have. I asked what he had said and he replied, "A boy on a buggy bike." I had a buggy pushchair for my dolls and I liked the sound of a buggy bike. So that's all I went on about. I wanted a buggy bike. My first two-wheeler was always known as my buggy bike. I was very happy with it, as it had a basket for my dolls, but I never could understand why the wheels were nothing like those on my dolls' buggy pushchair.

***

I knew the names of all my dad's work mates. I used to question him each evening about who he'd seen and who had used different pieces of machinery. My first question to my dad each night was, "Did you go on the dumper today?" I thought that was a really funny name for a piece of machinery.

I was probably five or six when my dad's mate Andy came on the weekends to build a stone path and some stone steps, leading off the main concrete path and down into the orchard. I always enjoyed talking to anyone who came to our house, and Andy always talked to me, asking me questions and answering mine. Therefore, it became my tradition, when Andy was working, to take my little stool, place it on the main concrete path out of the way, sit myself down and talk to him. He must have had a lot of patience, as I used to introduce him to all my dolls, then test him on their names!

Andy would disappear at dinner time and come back afterwards. I wish I could forget this part, but apparently it caused great hilarity when, one day, I asked him, "Why do you talk funny after dinner?" Unbeknownst to me, he used to like a drink at dinner time, but thankfully he saw the funny side to my question.

***

I spent as much time outside as possible. We had a lot of outside space so, if I wasn't on the swing or hanging upside down on one of the bars that went along either end of the swing frame, or up in one of the trees, I was usually riding around on something. One of the things I had was a pedal go-cart. It was great fun to ride round and round the concrete bit at the front of the house, usually singing at the top of my voice. I think it was easy to forget that I was blind, as I somehow was able to miss the fence and various walls as I rode around. The wheels were made from hard plastic, which made it quite noisy, too. That was probably the reason I never heard one of the neighbours come down the path one day. His daughters were about the same age as me, so he probably expected me to either stop, or go around him, as he stepped off the path and onto the area where I was riding. I didn't stop, nor did I go around him. Apparently it was only at the last moment when he jumped out of the way just in time! I don't think he   realised I was completely unaware that he was there.

***

Riding around at the front of the house was fine, but riding down the drive was more difficult. I could do it, but I couldn't get up any decent speed, as it was easy to come off the drive and go down quite a steep slope. I was about seven when I asked my dad to run beside me, so I could go down the drive. We set off and all was well. Remember those noisy wheels? I didn't hear Dad telling me to stop. I thought he was still with me as I came off the drive and onto the grass. Down the slope I went until I stopped, in the middle of the pampas grass! I had no idea where I'd ended up and when he finally caught up with me, Dad's response was his usual one of surprise, "Dearo!", said in a very drawn-out three syllable way.

***

One of my favourite things to do was to go into the woods with my dad and go on the rope swing. It was hanging from a huge beech tree, which seemed to be growing in the bank. The tree had been there so long, some of its roots were sticking out enough to sit on. Each time we went there, Dad would pull on the swing to test it, then lift me onto it. It was just a single rope with a stick going across at the bottom, which you sat on with a leg on either side of the rope. I still remember how smooth that stick felt, from many years of use and being out in all weathers. Dad would pull me up the bank, then let me swing out, the wind blowing my hair out behind me. It felt so freeing to swing like that. I remember looking down and seeing the tops of the trees further down the bank. I could spend ages just swinging around in all directions. I don't think Mum knew at the time how high I was going, but I was fearless.

***

Another time, after I'd abseiled down a tree at an organised event, I told my dad I wanted to abseil in the woods. This wasn't really an option, so Dad said we could abseil down a steep bank into a quarry. Off we went into the woods, taking a long rope with us. Dad looped the rope around a huge tree, then tied the other end around my waist. I was kind of scared of what I might find at the bottom, but I had to try it. Stepping cautiously backwards, I began my descent. It was quite a steep slope, but in no time at all I was at the bottom. Dad was still working the rope on the tree as I made my way back up again. Once I reached the top, I insisted it was Dad's turn. Thankfully he trusted me to work the rope, as I helped him to lower himself down into the quarry, then pulled him back up.

***

I had many adventures on space hoppers and roller skates, but when I was about eleven, I acquired a skateboard. I wasn't much good on it really. I was fine on the flat, but I wanted to go down the bank from the lawn at the top, down into the orchard. I could just about manage to stay standing up as I rode down the smallest end of the bank, but when I wanted to try out the steeper part, I decided it was safer sitting down.

 Dad was with me at the time and he helped line me up, making sure I wasn't heading for any trees. I had a few successful rides down the bank, until the time when I must have gone slightly off course. I was happily flying along when I heard Dad's urgent shout, "tree stump!" In a fraction of a second, I realised that if I ran into the tree stump, it would hurt! So I did what I thought was the quickest way of stopping. I slapped both feet down on the ground on either side of the skateboard and stood up. Where did I end up? Right on top of the tree stump! I think my dad was too shocked to speak for a moment, and I couldn't believe I'd actually managed to stop myself and stand up all in one movement...on the tree stump, of all places! That was another occasion for the three-syllable "Dearo!"

4

I loved spending time with Granddad. He would help me make things, cut out strings of dancing dolls for me, answer all sorts of random questions, and he even agreed to be a traffic and travel reporter when I had a pretend radio station, which was actually just a tape recorder. He would play ball with us kids, or blow up rubber gloves until they were so huge that I would run outside, in case they burst! He would also make massive snowballs and snowmen with us on the rare occasions that we got enough snow.

I never liked scary stories, but I used to ask Granddad to tell me stories about thunder bolts which came into the house. I wouldn't be scared, because Granddad was there with me. Even real thunder storms were less scary when he was there.

We sometimes went for long walks, and if you went for a ride in the car with Granddad, you never knew where you would end up, as he liked to see where different roads led. I think the joke was that he usually ended up in a farm yard!

Whereas Grandma liked to stand outside and talk to the neighbours, or go down the street and stop to talk to everyone, Granddad was quieter with people outside of the family.

I remember one evening when my auntie, uncle, and cousins were staying at Grandma and Granddad's, I wanted to go out and look at the moon. Granddad took me outside and let me sit on top of the gate, one of my favourite places. My auntie and uncle's dog, Dinky, must have followed us out there and was wandering around the front garden.

As we were admiring the moon, I heard someone walk up the path in front of the houses. As the person passed, Granddad said, "Hello Eddie." He was the man who lived next door.

Dinky had now realised someone was passing, and he started barking. Without hesitation, Granddad said quite loudly, "Shut up Eddie!"

I immediately burst out laughing! I think Granddad hoped Eddie hadn't heard, but he was so embarrassed, he lifted me off the gate and we went back into the house rather quickly! As you can imagine, six- or seven-year-old me couldn't wait to tell all the family what had happened. I was laughing so much, though, it took a while. They all saw the funny side, and even Granddad laughed about it too.

***

It was a particularly hot summer, and I was spending quite a bit of time at Grandma and Granddad's house, because Mum was working. I was intrigued by the thermometer on the wall outside, especially as Granddad would give us regular temperature updates. One day it was very hot. Granddad announced that the temperature was in the nineties and might reach one hundred later in the afternoon.

A short time later, he found me outside, sitting under the patio table. He could see something was wrong and when he asked me, I burst into tears and said, "If it gets to one hundred, we'll boil!" He then explained that there were two temperature scales and the thermometer he had was Fahrenheit, which had a much higher number for boiling point. I was very relieved, but felt rather silly!

***

One day my cousin Martyn and I wanted to make toffee. I don't know what happened, but it didn't set. Grandma said we'd cooked it too much, but we weren't about to give up on it that easily. I think Granddad had been looking forward to some toffee as well, as he didn't give up on it either. First, he put it on the kitchen window sill where it was cooler, but still it didn't set. Next, it went in the fridge, still with no success. Finally he suggested putting it in the oven. We had nothing to lose, so in it went. It didn't taste like toffee when it came out, but it did set and it was actually really nice!

***

Granddad always seemed to understand my desire to design and create things, so when I was a teenager, we worked together to design the built-in wardrobe in my bedroom at home. It had shelves just the right size for the various things I needed to use them for. Every bit of space was used. I remember being really happy when Granddad started to build it. He never did get to finish it, but I always thought of him when I used it.

***

I always enjoyed eating at Grandma and Granddad's house. Sometimes Granddad would make proper chips and make a cone from greaseproof paper to put them in. Sometimes he made "scallops", which were thinly sliced potato rounds cooked like chips. Grandma made the best lasagna and I could never get enough of it.

Grandma sometimes cooked some funny combinations of things, though. I remember asking one day, "What's for dinner, Grandma?" She replied, "Bacon, egg," to both of which I replied, "mmm!" She went on to say, "Mashed potato," which I think I pulled a face at, before she finished, "And cabbage."

"Cabbage?" I squeaked! Even Granddad commented that it didn't really go. I like cabbage, but not with fried egg!

Grandma's reply was, "Oh well!"

I used to love to help Grandma prepare Sunday tea. Everyone in the family who lived near enough would get together at Grandma and Granddad's for Sunday tea. Cutting things up and putting things in dishes was always so much fun! I never minded how many trips I made to and from the living room table.

Grandma liked her food. On the rare occasion that she wasn't able to finish what she had on her plate, she always said, "I think my eyes were bigger than my belly!" That always made me laugh.

5

During my childhood we always had a dog. Sebastian was there long before I came along and according to Mum, he used to guard my pram while I was outside. No one could approach me without first having spoken to Mum.

Sebastian was getting quite old, so when I was five, Mum and Dad decided to get a puppy for me. I remember us making quite a long journey to go and get the golden Labrador, who I named Bloo. Note the spelling, I insisted it had to be that way. He was really light in colour, and he seemed to have big dark eyes. Bloo and I were instantly friends. When I was playing with my dolls, he was there. When I was on the swing, he was always somewhere nearby. The only thing I wouldn't let him near were balls, or my space hopper, as I think he used to burst them with excitement!

We lived right near the woods, so Bloo didn't have to get used to the lead when we took him there. However, if we were walking on the roads, Bloo liked to make sure we were walking at a good pace! So, I decided to do what I called "lead training". I put the lead on Bloo and off we went, up the path to the garage, then on up the drive. Up and down we went, many times. I would then make him sit at the edge of the drive and wait, as though we were crossing a road. He was only allowed to move forward when I said so. Each and every time we did this, he never once pulled me. He was as gentle as could be. Our neighbours used to watch our adventures, as their house was sort of over to the side, halfway between our house and our gate.

We had an area opposite the garage, which had about a four-foot drop off of it onto the lawn below. It seems that one day, I misjudged where I was and was getting near the drop. Bloo got between me and the drop and moved me over, making sure I didn't fall off.

Bloo was taken from our garden when I was eleven years old. He unfortunately got knocked down on the road while trying to return home. For a few months we didn't have a dog, until Ben arrived from a rescue centre.

***

Ben was a black and white Border Collie and seemed to have the most enormous tail! He was six months old and didn't always know how he should behave, but he soon learned. He was a clever dog, as we soon found out he could open doors. He would jump up to the handle and push down on it, pushing the door open. The problem was, though, that he could let himself out through the front door as it opened outwards, then come in through the back door, as it opened inwards; but he never learned to shut the doors behind him!

Ben was not a fan of thunder. He alerted us to its coming long before we ever heard it. No dog could flop down on the floor and sigh in such a way as he did, as if to say, "It's thundering again." I remember one afternoon when Mum and I were going to visit Grandma and Granddad. We heard the thunder in the distance, so decided to take Ben with us. It was getting nearer as we ran up to the car. Just before I reached the car, there was a loud clap, right overhead. I'm not a fan of thunder either, so I opened the car door and jumped in! I was not expecting Ben to jump in at exactly the same time as I did, though. I never let the dog sit by my feet, but somehow, Ben and I jumped into the car in one movement. He tucked himself in by my feet, even tucking his tail in quickly enough for me to shut the door without hesitation! Mum said she'd never seen anything quite like it!

***

How is it that dogs can tell the time? Both Ben and Sheba, the dog we had next, knew when our neighbours had their cup of tea and biscuit at eleven O'clock. They both also knew that if they were up by the wall, they would get a biscuit too. One day, Ben was lying in a different place. He was stretched out across the garage doorway. It was a sliding door and we left it open most of the time. Even after his biscuit, Ben went back to the garage. Mum wondered why he was lying there, looking down at the house. Eventually, after most of the day had passed, Mum realised what was happening when she saw Ben chase away a magpie. When she went to look in the garage, a magpie had pecked its way into the sack of dry dog food and helped itself. Ben had realised and had been guarding the now open sack! He never hurt the magpie, he just made sure it wasn't going to share any more of his food.

***

When I had rabbits, we would let them run about on the lawn. Catching them, though, was not easy. They are able to move at quite a speed, and just when you think you'll get one, it bounces under a bush and you can't reach it. Then we discovered Ben could help us. Having four legs, he could obviously keep up with the rabbits more easily. He would know when we were trying to catch one and would gently hold it down with his paw, just to keep it still enough to catch. He would then look at us and squeak, as if to say, "Come on, I've got it for you." They were not frightened by him at all as they were often nose to nose through the wire door of the hutches.

**

Sheba was another good thunder alert dog. Unfortunately, she would start shaking and get behind the settee. If you were sat on it, it felt more like an earth quake than a thunder storm!

Sheba's hate of thunder was equaled by her love of all things spherical. She loved balls. If there was no ball to be found, an apple would suffice. Whenever my dad came to visit me, Sheba recognised his van. He was working on a site near a park and would often find balls lying around. Knowing how much Sheba liked them, he would bring them for her. Sheba went straight to his van, searching for them. She didn't like giving up when he hadn't found one that week.

**

Once Mum and I moved from the house where I'd grown up, Sheba lived with Mum. One Christmas I was around Mum's, wrapping up presents—on the landing, of all places—when I dropped the sellotape through the bars of the banister. It rolled and bounced its way down the stairs and landed who knew where. I followed it down the stairs but didn't know where to begin searching. I think I said something like, "Where's it gone, Sheba?" and, seeming to know what I wanted, Sheba got out of her bed and walked across the kitchen. When I followed her, I found the Sellotape there, right by her nose. She had led me right to it.

6

The house I grew up in had three bedrooms. The spare room was always referred to as the back bedroom. The back bedroom wardrobe wasn't used for clothes. There were no shelves or rails. It was a built-in wardrobe with sliding doors, and it stretched the width of the room. It was a wonderful place to keep all sorts of things, mostly my toys and games.

I loved to go up and see what I could find in there, sorting and tidying things as I went, although I usually had a different way of organising each time.

One day when I was about ten, I was looking for something in the back bedroom wardrobe. I have no idea what it was now, but I know a whole pile of games, boxes, and bags decided to sort of create an avalanche! I tried desperately to put them back in order, but I didn't have enough hands. If I moved from my position, half crouching, half in and half out of the wardrobe, the whole lot would slide and go everywhere!

So I decided to call my mum. I didn't know where in the house she was, so didn't call too loudly. Only, when I called "Mum!" all I heard through the open window was "quack!" from one of the neighbour's ducks. The second time I called a little louder, "Mum!" This time the response was "quack quack!" I wanted to laugh, but stopping the piles of stuff from sliding was getting urgent. I tried a little louder and was answered by "quack quack, quack"! Now it was really urgent! I took a deep breath and shouted "Mum!!!" as loud as I could. This time the duck broke into a burst of quacking and all I could do was burst out laughing.

I don't think I've ever been answered by a duck before or since that day, but it was hilarious.

7

I started play-school at the age of two. It was a scary place for me, as there were children there with all sorts of disabilities and most of them couldn't talk. They would also run into me on bikes and other such toys! One good thing came out of being there, though: I met Berta and we have been friends ever since. She helped me find my way around, while I talked nonstop to her! We also shared the same taxi on the way to and from Play-school.

At the age of four, while Berta went to the local school, I went to a school in Quedgeley, Gloucester, where there was a unit attached where braille and other resources could be provided. I had a very good experience at that mainstream school, my only complaint being that I had to travel about 45 minutes or more, morning and evening, to get to and from school, which meant I couldn't easily meet up with friends.

As you can imagine, these long journeys each day gave chance for many different things to happen, especially when I shared the taxi with others. I probably used to drive everyone mad for the first couple of years, as I seem to remember spending most of the journey singing! I also remember a lady Grandma worked with telling me she often waved to me, as she'd seen the taxi drive through one of the villages on the way to Gloucester. I wanted to wave back, but had no idea when she'd be around. So for some time, I would start waving wildly as we got to that village and keep waving until I was sure we'd left it!

***

I think I was about nine years old when we started picking up two brothers who went to the same school as me. They were only in the taxi about fifteen minutes, but we knew they were there! I think they were about seven and five at the time, and if they were not arguing, they were crying. So I came up with a plan. Whichever of them was the best behaved each morning could listen to a song on my Walkman when we got to the speed bumps! This actually worked amazingly well! I dread to think how bossy I was, telling them they needed to behave, else they wouldn't listen to a song, but they never seemed to mind.

***

At the age of eleven, I went to a mainstream secondary school. However, instead of attaching the unit to the secondary school all my friends from Primary school were going to, I had to go to a different part of Gloucester and make new friends. I was only at the school for a year, but I think it seemed to be a year of floods! One day the road was flooded so badly that I spent the night at a friend's house, while another day I had a very different adventure.

I seem to remember hearing the thunder rumbling during our geography lesson. The rain soon came and was still falling when it was time to leave for home after that lesson. At that time, there were two brothers who drove me to and from school, one in the morning and the other in the afternoon. I liked them both, but the one who usually drove me in the afternoon had worked with Granddad, so I thought he was the best! On this particular day, they had swapped and the less talkative of the two was driving me home. The roads were very wet and when we got to a certain point, he announced there was a lot of water on the road. I remember him driving slowly into it, then we stopped.

I knew that the river Severn runs alongside the main road to Gloucester and that in some places it's quite close. I imagined that the water on the road was overflowing from the river. I also knew that the Severn has a strong current, so I was terrified. I'm not sure why, but the driver decided to get out of the car. Unfortunately, as he opened his door, a lorry went by in the other direction, causing water to swoosh into the car, then the car itself bounced! At this point, I was sure we were going to end up in the river and I burst into tears! I was on my own in the car and didn't know how far away the river was.

Then my door opened and a fireman was there. He actually carried me out of the car and up someone's drive, where the man who was driving me was now waiting. We were invited into someone's house and I remember being offered a drink. I don't know when I asked if the car would end up in the river, but when I did, I was told that it was nowhere near the river. The flood water was just from the rain. I felt a bit silly at this point, but not as much as I did when there was a photo in the local paper of me being carried by the fireman!

**

For four years I attended a boarding school and they were the longest four years of my life! The school was about an hour's drive away, so I insisted on coming home every weekend. Most people who went home on the weekend returned to school on Sunday evenings, but eventually I was able to go back on a Monday morning. This was how it was when I was sixteen and doing my GCSEs. I was always at school long before I needed to be, apart from once. It was the day of one of my exams, and as we were travelling towards Worcester, we heard that there had been an accident on the motorway. I tried to stay calm as we sat in the traffic queue, but I was constantly wondering what would happen if I missed my exam! I hate being late for anything! I knew that if I had to go into my exam late, everyone would know about it. I think I sat there twisting my fingers into knots! We would move a bit, and then stop. For some time, we didn't move at all. I don't remember whether we finally got passed, or whether we came off the motorway and joined all the other traffic queuing to go the other way. The time I was usually at school had long since passed. The time for assembly came and went. By the time we reached the school, I knew my exam had started.

I remember running into the house and dropping my belongings in the hallway. I then raced across to the main building and ran straight to the gym, where the exam was taking place. I didn't know how one was supposed to enter an exam late, so I remember opening the gym door slightly and poking my head inside. Thankfully, one of the teachers spotted me, and everyone was relieved that I was finally there! I'm not sure how well I concentrated on that exam, I was just relieved to have got there.

8

I had a lot of fun with my cousins when we were growing up. Three of them lived nearby, which meant we got to see a lot of each other. We also had many adventures at Grandma and Granddad's house.

One summer our mothers were both working, so the four of us spent the days at Grandma and Granddad's. We spent hours on roller skates, or playing all sorts of games. There was a brilliant path that ran down the front of the houses, which was a great place to play. I only nearly ran over someone once on my roller skates, but realised just in time and landed myself in the hedge to avoid her!

We also found it a good place to go down while sitting on skateboards. Martyn was by far the bravest of us, as by that time, I was more aware of danger! Usually Martyn would fly down the path on the little skateboard, while I followed with one or both of the younger girls, on the big skateboard. One day Martyn suggested that he and I go down together on the bigger skateboard. I knew I couldn't go fast on my own, as I could end up flying down over the bank onto the road, or hitting a post or a scary wire fence. So I took him up on his offer. I agreed to go on the condition that we only went as far as the end house. I didn't want to turn the sharp corner at the bottom and go along the even-narrower path that was overgrown, as there were also steps at the end. I knew you could pick up quite a speed while traveling down there.

So, we went right to the top. Martyn sat in front and I sat behind him, trying not to hang on to him too tightly, but tight enough that I wouldn't fall off! I remember tucking my hair down the back of my top, so it wouldn't get caught in the fence or anything as we passed, then off we went!

We sped past the first two houses, turned right slightly, then left, then left again, following the path as it made its way around the turning point below, passing three more houses as we went. After turning right once more, we were on the straight path and could pick up even more speed! On past the next five houses we whizzed! I knew we would be coming to where we had to stop soon, but we didn't. Instead Martyn skillfully turned us around the corner and onto the bit of path I'd said I didn't want to go on. On and on we went, I knew we had to be coming to the steps soon, so thought that surely Martyn would stop us. I was kind of excited and scared at the same time! I thought about trying to stop us myself, but didn't dare!

Then it happened. We sort of went ba-boing ba-boing ba-boing ba-boing ba-boing!!! We successfully bounced our way down all five steps and Martyn stopped us at the bottom. How we both stayed on the skateboard I'll never know!

I think Martyn exclaimed, "That was good, wasn't it!" with a huge grin on his face. I think my response was something like, "no! You idiot!" before walking back up the path in a strop! I had secretly sort of enjoyed it, although I had been scared. I also admired his bravery and skateboard-steering skills. I think even he was surprised how successful it had been!

**

When I was in my late teens, I borrowed Sophie's bike to see if I could still ride one. I chose to give it a go in the evening, when I could see best. The concrete area I used to ride on wasn't big enough for me to do that anymore, so off I went up the path and onto the lawn. It was quite a good sized lawn and I was getting quite confident that I hadn't forgotten how to ride, when there was a "swoosh!" I immediately heard Martyn burst out laughing from where he had been watching down by the house. I had managed to directly hit one of the shrubs growing there, snapping it right off! Martyn couldn't get in the house fast enough to tell Mum, who, thankfully, found it funny. It was the shrub that was almost dead anyway, so I said I put it out of its misery! With all the space on the lawn, I don't know how I managed to hit it.

***

Even though Martyn is four and a half years younger than me, we spent a lot of time together. We went for several walks, sometimes in the woods, or down to Grandma and Granddad's, or even the three miles each way to Lydney through the back roads. We often ended up covered with mud, as I think he liked to find out where different paths in the woods led. I remember one afternoon, we'd walked to Lydney and got something to eat from the fish and chip shop. We'd called in at someone's house for a cup of tea, then started on our way home. Most of the journey was on the back roads where there was hardly any traffic. I recall us stopping and Martyn was telling me about a rabbit hopping down the road in front of us. We were able to watch it for ages, as we were so quiet.

I don't know why, but as we got to the steep hill where the trees on either side of the road met above us, making it very dark, we decided to tell each other scary stories. All of a sudden a pigeon flapped really noisily overhead, making us jump so much that we stood in the middle of the road, hanging on to each other! I think we gave up on the scary stories after that.

***

In the orchard was a pear tree. One year there were quite a few pears on the tree, but it was difficult to get them. Mum said the tree was brittle, so climbing it wasn't an option. There also wasn't the room to get a ladder in there. I don't know who came up with the idea of me sitting on Martyn's shoulders, but we gave it a go. By this time, Martyn had long since overtaken me in size. He crouched down and I got onto his shoulders. As he went to get up, the two of us nearly went headfirst into the tree—which as you can imagine, caused much hilarity. Mum was then trying to direct me to the pears. I think it was more hard work for all of us than it was worth, but we got a few.

9

I think I can only describe this section as "blind moments"! I've had a few in my time.

It took me until I was about eleven to ask my dad a question which was puzzling me. On our weekly trip into Gloucester, whilst he drove up floor after floor to find a space in the multi-storey car park, I finally asked, "Why is it that when we go out of the car park and you pay the man, you always say "Thank you Mate!", and you've paid him, but when we go into the car park and he gives you the ticket, you never thank him?"

After Dad finally stopped laughing, he explained that you took the ticket from a machine on the way in. I had thought the man was sitting in the middle of the road, between the way in and the way out, handing out tickets, then collecting the money. It had never occurred to me that there was a machine.

Let's just say that my dad never let me forget that. Even now, all these years later, when he drives into the car park and takes the ticket from the machine, he says, "thank you mate!"

***

Thankfully, I'm not the only one who does daft things, as the next one was my closest friend, Alex. Alex's parents took us both on holiday to a caravan on a lovely site. Within seconds, we could be on the pebbly beach. Alex and I spent a lot of time on the beach, enjoying the sea, walking barefoot on the pebbles, which did cause Alex to end up on her knees a few times, and sun bathing.

Anyway, one day we went with Alex's parents, Jeff and Iris, to the café on the site. I think we went upstairs, where there was an area to sit outside as well as inside.

I was at the counter with Iris, while Jeff and Alex went to get a table. Jeff left Alex at the table and came to tell us something. He went back to Alex, but soon returned to us, laughing so much he couldn't tell us why.

He'd told Alex there was a seat by her, before coming to the counter the first time. However, when he got back to her, Alex was happily seated on the table! True, it was a low table, and so Alex had made herself quite comfortable on it, thinking it was some sort of funny bench. She said, "He said to sit by there, but the one by there was higher than the other, so I sat on the lower one."

***

I love getting the washing out on the line. On this particular day, as I usually did, I hung the washing on the line and left the laundry basket and peg bag on the bench.

When it was time to take the washing in, the peg bag was still there, but the basket was nowhere to be seen. The wind had picked up a bit during the day, so I guessed my basket had blown off the bench. I looked around near the bench, but it was nowhere to be found. I then ventured further into the garden. My back garden isn't very big at all, but there was still grass on part of it at the time and it's very difficult to tell which bit of grass you've searched, and which you haven't.

After several minutes, I gave up and took the washing into the house in my arms. I then went back for another look.

I could hear children playing on the green area at the back of the houses and I even considered going out to see if any of them would come and help me find my basket. I didn't really know any of them well, so gave up on that thought. There is a wooden fence around my garden that's about six feet high, so I didn't think it was likely that the plastic basket had gone up that high and over the fence, but I couldn't be sure.

I started trying to work out which direction the wind was blowing, and after about ten minutes I eventually found it, right at the bottom corner.

I didn't want to risk that happening again, so ever since then, I've left the unused pegs in the basket to weigh it down and, so far, I haven't had to go on a basket hunt since.

***

Just the other day Alex came over and we spent the afternoon on the swing seat in my back garden. I have a little table out there, and when Alex went to put her phone on it, she bumped the mug she'd used earlier. I heard a sort of swoosh, and a thud, so thought it had tipped out its contents, but Alex said it was empty. We both searched and searched. It sounded like it hit the wooden fence, but that was quite a distance away and we couldn't find it anywhere. We then checked around the legs of the swing, which are also made of wood, which would have explained what we heard. Still we couldn't find it. Eventually, I wondered if it had gone in the flowerpot at the side of the swing. Alex looked, and that's where it was. The swoosh I'd heard was the mug going through the leaves and flowers as it landed in the pot.

***

Just before Christmas, I came downstairs one morning and went to put my phone on the coffee table. Thankfully, I had my slipper socks on my feet, because as my toes went slightly under the table, I stepped on something kind of squidgy and bouncy! Immediately I knew it was a slug. I remember stepping on one outside once before, thankfully with shoes on, however this time it was in the house.

I carefully walked, with my toes in the air, to get some toilet paper from the downstairs loo. I was dreading having to look for all the slime trails it was sure to have made. I guessed it must have come in the front door on my shoe, from where it had made its way from the doormat, where I left my shoes, into the living room and under the table.

I got a nice big handful of paper and headed back to the living room, still with my toes in the air, as I didn't want to spread the slime that was probably on the underside of my slipper sock. I arranged the toilet paper around my hand, took a deep breath, then bent to pick up the offensive squidgy slug. I grabbed it quickly, then burst out laughing as I felt through the paper the shape of a suction hook! I had been using them to put up some of my Christmas decorations. It seems one had obviously bounced away from me and landed under the table! I have to say I was relieved it wasn't a slug.

***

My friend Helen and I met for lunch one day in a café. It was quite busy in there and after ordering at the counter, we took our things to the table. The tables were quite small and after a bit of rearranging, we got sorted. I was intending to pour my tea, but didn't want to pick up the wrong teapot. Trying not to handle the pot too much, in case it wasn't mine, I asked, "Is this my teapot?" Helen said quite calmly, "That's a plant!" We then both burst out laughing! I have to admit, though, the plant pot did look like the teapot. I'm just glad I didn't try pouring it into my cup, but if I'd actually picked it up, I would have realised it wasn't hot enough!

***

I began this section with a story about me and Dad in the car park, so I'll end it with another. Just last week, we went into Gloucester to find quite a few spaces taken in the car park. Dad parked in what he called "a different kind of space", and told me I wouldn't have much room to get out. I'm quite used to him parking in tight spaces, so didn't think too much about it. I carefully opened the door and slithered out sideways. Realising I had a bit more room than I thought, I must have put my foot forward a bit, straight into a freezing cold puddle of water! I said something like, "Yuck! There's a puddle!" As Dad came around to where I was now squelching in my sandals at the back of the car, my first question was, "Is it clean water?" I was imagining all sorts of yucky things that might be in there. Thankfully it was clean. It was a three inch channel running along by the wall for drainage or something. Dad thinks they must have washed the floor of the car park down.

I don't know about Doctor Foster who went to Gloucester, but I know I was squidging around in my sandals for a while. I'm just glad I wasn't wearing shoes, as they would have taken longer to dry! I couldn't get the nursery rhyme out of my head all day!

"Doctor Foster went to Gloucester in a shower of rain.

He stepped in a puddle right up to his middle and never went there again!"

10

My first cooking disaster happened when I was about twelve years old. My friend Lesley was at my house and we decided to make popcorn while Mum was out. That would have been fine, but I had this idea that it would be good to make a sauce to go over it.

We popped the corn, then, not having much experience of cooking, I decided we needed to use butter and sugar. I don't remember exactly what happened, but somehow it burnt to the bottom of the saucepan. I don't even remember us eating the popcorn, although I'm sure we did. However I do remember us trying to scrub the saucepan. We took it in turns. One would scrub and scrub until our arm felt like it might fall off, while the other watched at the living room window for Mum to come down the drive. It was still marked when she did return home. It was only then we gave up the scrubbing and gabbled as fast as possible at her as soon as she came through the door, telling her we'd tried to get the saucepan clean. She wasn't the slightest bit bothered about it. Somehow she managed to get it clean—by boiling potato peelings in it, I think. We used it for years afterwards, so it must have been okay.

***

Another disaster Lesley and I had happened while we were making toasted cheese sandwiches under the grill at the top of the oven. Having quite small hands, I always struggled with large oven gloves. It was hard to feel what I was doing with all that extra squishiness sticking out far beyond the ends of my fingers. I think I was looking for the grill pan to pull it out—I don't know why we didn't put a handle on it. Then Lesley suddenly said, "Lou! The oven glove's on fire!" I ran to the sink, threw it off my hand, and ran water on it. There was always a bit of a hole at the end of it from then on, but it was still usable.

***

When I had my own kitchen, I had different kinds of disasters. I'm generally quite organised and usually remember what's what, but I guess I sometimes forget. These days, there are wonderful apps I can use on my phone which will read text on packaging, but not when I first lived here.

One day I decided to have a buttered roll with some soup. I'm not one of these people who is able to butter a roll delicately: I sort of half spread it on one side of the roll, then squish the two halves together. This means I probably eat more butter than necessary, but as Grandma always said, "Oh well!" I was looking forward to my roll, but when I bit into it, something was not right. It did not have a nice buttery taste. I tried dipping it into the soup, but it was no better. I'd heard Mum say that she didn't like unsalted butter, so I thought I must have bought that by mistake. I remember thinking, "If that's unsalted butter, you can keep it!" I took the rest of the pack to Mum's house for identification later that day. It wasn't unsalted butter at all. It was lard! I'd forgotten I'd bought some to make pastry and both butter and lard come wrapped in paper.

***

There are four smoke alarms in my house. I've since learnt that some are smoke alarms, while some are heat sensors. They are all connected into the electricity, so when one goes off, it's squeak central as they all join in. I'm guessing having an alarm in the kitchen is sensible in one way, but not when it goes off when you cook toast. I don't overcook my toast and I always emptied the crumbs out of the bottom. Making toast became a nightmare. By the time I'd flapped a towel wildly at the alarm until my arms ached, I'd gone off the idea of toast.

One day I was feeling brave. I was waiting for the alarm to go off as the toast cooked, but I was relieved when, by the time the toast popped up, all was quiet. I sighed with relief as I took the toast out of the toaster, then it happened. I heard wild high-pitched squeaking which made me jump so much that I threw the toast over my shoulder and across the kitchen! I never got to enjoy my toast that day either.

***

Internet shopping is a wonderful thing. I love being able to have a really good look at what food I can buy and take my time deciding what to get. Most of the time I know what things are when they arrive, but sometimes it can be a bit confusing if I haven't ordered something before, so I don't know what it will look like when it comes.

One day last year, while putting my groceries away, I found the most yucky squidgy thing I've ever met! It was in a plastic packet and there was loads of liquid slopping about in there. In the liquid was a squidgy blob, which reminded me of an eyeball, or a dead fish. I was convinced I must have been given this thing by mistake. I didn't even want to handle it, so instead of using an app to identify it, I took it around to Mum's house, as I had groceries to take to her anyway. Holding it by its corner, I almost threw it into her hands asking, "What is it? It reminds me of a dead fish!" Once she'd stopped laughing, she told me it was mozzarella. I'd ordered it to go in macaroni cheese, but I never expected it to look like that! I dreaded having to open it and get rid of all that sloppiness, then deal with the squidginess; but when I did use it, it wasn't so bad after all! I've even bought it again since!

11

My cousin Sophie and I had lots of fun when we were younger. We always enjoyed singing together, and I remember us trying to write a play once. We used to go for lots of walks, especially when Mum was working in one particular place. Sophie and I used to time our walk so we could go and meet Mum from work. It was probably over three miles, more like four if we went the long way around, which we often liked to do. Somehow we always seemed to meet a huge tractor in the narrowest part of the lanes and had to run to a field gateway, as there wasn't much space to pass.

On the way to meet Mum, we would pass some pigs. Sophie always had to lean over the fence and talk to them! I confess I stood well back, as I wasn't keen on all that grunting and squealing!

One day, we decided to go for a walk. We walked down into Blakeney, then around the back roads. When we were on the last stretch of the back roads, there was suddenly a lot of mud. We were feeling a bit lazy and didn't want to go all the way back the way we'd come, so we decided to make our way carefully through the mud! It got deeper and deeper, squidgier and squidgier! It nearly pulled our shoes off a few times and the slurping noises it was making were not nice at all. I'm older by about six years, so I suggested we should maybe turn around. Sophie insisted we were nearly there, so we might as well carry on. So, on we went. I told myself we couldn't sink too deep, as there was a solid road underneath, but I wondered if the road had maybe disappeared when we kept getting our feet stuck. I could hear a tractor in a nearby field and even wondered how easily we could get the attention of the driver if we got really stuck!

Thankfully we finally made it through. I was so relieved, but I knew our shoes would tell the story! We went to Grandma's house and cleaned them off, then relaxed with a cup of tea before walking the two and a half miles home, with relatively clean shoes!

***

I met that muddy area again a couple of years later when Mum, Grandma, and I decided to go for a walk around the back roads. It was a nice afternoon and we had Ben, the Border collie, with us. We were on the last stretch when Mum announced that it was really muddy and we'd have to walk on the bank. This was fine: I walked along behind Mum and Grandma followed me. We were passing the same area Sophie and I had got stuck in, but I'd never thought of walking on the bank back then. I don't even think I knew there was one!

All went well, until we came to a channel which had been cut out of the bank to let the water drain off the field. At that point I said I'd rather go back the long way, but Mum insisted we could cross it. First Mum stepped out onto a stone in the middle. If we stepped off that stone, the water and mud would be above our ankles, so she balanced there, while trying to direct me. Ben seemed to know we needed help. He stood in the water so Mum could hold onto him with one hand to balance herself, while I hung onto her other arm, trying to work out where I had to put my foot. There was not enough room on the stone for four feet, so once I had my first foot on there, Mum had to cross the rest of the way to the bank on the other side. I then had to get my other foot onto the stone, before taking a huge stride across onto the bank to join Mum. I'm sure people with longer legs don't have so much trouble!

Once we were on the bank, Mum turned to Grandma and said, "I'll just take Lou along here a bit further, then I'll come back and help you." Grandma agreed, but a few seconds later, we heard splash squish squish! Grandma said instantly, "I knew I'd slip, I washed my coat and all!" She'd decided not to wait for Mum's help and had ended up on her side in the mud! All three of us were laughing. I remember Grandma saying, "I've got to walk through the street like this!"

***

Another time Sophie and I walked down to Grandma's and decided to come home the last part of the way through the woods. We seemed to be getting higher and higher, then eventually Sophie realised we were at the top of a really high bank. We needed to get down it somehow and there was only one way. I followed Sophie as we made our way, on our hands and knees, down the steep bank, which was probably as high as a house, if not higher. The aim was to first get to the tree which was part the way down, but Sophie ended up sliding too soon and got to the bottom very quickly! She then had to direct me from where she was, to get to the shallower part, with fewer big rocks in it.

I successfully got to the tree, then wondered how to get down the final steepest part. I was about seventeen or eighteen, which meant that I was also much more aware of danger than I was as a child. Sophie said the best way to get down was on my backside. I sat down, but it took a while for me to let go of the tree I was clinging to. Then off I went, bouncing over all sorts of things until I landed at the bottom. I was relieved to be down there and even more relieved I hadn't put a hole in my clothes!

The funniest part was that when we got to my house Mum said, "I could hear you two out in the woods! Ben was listening to you as well." I think the dog would have joined us if Mum had told him to come and help us! I'd forgotten that the bit of woods we were in wasn't far from the back of our house, I'd also forgotten how sound travels through the woods.

12

Apparently, when we are asleep, we are supposed to be resting; only I'm not sure that's always the case with me. I'd been told I walked and talked in my sleep, but never really thought too much about it until I went to boarding school, where it was soon confirmed by the girls I shared a room with that I definitely talked in my sleep!

I always seemed to be the first to fall asleep at night, and a great source of amusement to the girls who were still awake and chatting was to talk to me and see if I would answer. I usually did.

They could ask me the time, I could look at my braille watch and tell them. They could ask me what day it was, I could answer correctly, even checking my watch to see if it was after midnight. They could ask me what homework we had, yes, I could answer that too.

The problem came when they started asking me questions when I was still awake. I had no way of proving I was awake and not asleep, as even getting out of bed and walking around the room wasn't enough to convince them. I think that the only thing that convinced them that I was really still awake was that I would get frustrated that they didn't believe me.

***

I was always afraid of walking in my sleep and going out of my room; but fortunately, I never did that—at least I don't think I did! One night, though, I dreamt that I had gone downstairs and for weeks afterward I was terrified I'd actually done it!

I didn't stop at sleep walking. One night I woke up to discover I'd changed from my night clothes into leggings. I'd even folded my nightie up tidily and put it in a drawer! I was terrified the fire alarm would go off as I struggled to find where I'd put my nightie since, let's just say, I was only half dressed.

So you may be wondering if I grew out of it all. The answer is no. When friends have stayed at my house, they've heard me talking or walking around. I'm not afraid I'll fall down the stairs or anything, as I seem to be too alert to do that.

***

Back a couple of years ago, it moved to a whole new level. I got into bed and realised I hadn't taken my earrings out. I should have taken them out and put them away properly, but I took them out and put them on the set of drawers by my bed.

I woke up in the night and wondered what was sticking in me. I'd only put the earrings back in! It may have been three in the morning, but I wasn't going to take any chances. I got up and put them away properly. Who knows how many times I would have put them back in otherwise! I think I had put one in backwards though, so is that a sign of being less alert than I thought, or is it a sign of even more sleep skill, as putting the earring in backwards required me to put the wing on the front of my ear instead of the back!

13

I'm not someone who often falls over things, but when I do, I do it in style!

The first of these incidents involved my friend Lesley. Our mothers have been friends for years and when we were about ten and eleven—Lesley is a year older than me—we, too, became friends. I think we were twelve and thirteen when this story happened. We had a set pattern for each weekend: Lesley would stay at my house on a Friday night, We would go to Gloucester with my dad on Saturday afternoon, then he would drop us both off at Lesley's house where I would stay Saturday night. This pattern went on for several years. On this particular day, Lesley and I had decided to dress the same. We both wore long red skirts, white tops, and black suede shoes with little heels. I think we felt very grown up. We'd gone into what we as teenagers called a "junk shop". We didn't want to look around in there, so we decided to wait for Dad outside. All I can say is that I wasn't concentrating. I sighed and stepped sideways in a sort of sulky strop, but I had a bit of a shock. We were standing at the top of a flight of five brick steps and as I stepped sideways, I stepped off the top step. I was hanging on to Lesley with my right hand and before we knew it, the two of us were flying down the steps to our left. We both ended up lying on our sides at the bottom in a very undignified heap, the height of embarrassment for a twelve- and thirteen-year-old! All these lovely kind people came rushing over to see if we were okay, but I just wanted to disappear into a hole! I remember banging my elbow, which hurt for months, but my main concern was that I'd lost my shoe! It turns out that Lesley had also lost a shoe. She found them both, her left and my right, lined up together on the bottom step!

**

I was a teenager when Mum asked me to go up into her bedroom to get something. As I usually did, I ran up the stairs and into her room. I kept running from the lower part of the room to the higher part, where I must have needed to go to get whatever it was she had asked for, but suddenly I was flying through the air. As I ran into the object I'd hit, I suddenly remembered that the portable gas fire was in Mum's bedroom. I knew it wasn't on, but I knew gas exploded. I screamed as I flew through the air, then I landed on top of the fire and sort of rolled off sideways.

Mum and my cousin Martyn came running up the stairs after hearing all the commotion. They couldn't get over how far I'd moved the fire from its original place.

Nothing exploded and I only had a bruise on my arm from landing on the fire. I think the fire had a dent in it from then on, though! I definitely saw the funny side of it, as did Mum and Martyn.

**

For the last two years of my time in boarding school, I shared a room with my best friend, Fiona. We went everywhere together and had a lot of fun. In some ways we were similar, although she is far more musically talented than I'll ever be, but in other ways we were very different. Everyone knew Fiona, but a lot of people didn't know me, as I was so quiet back then. The other difference was in how tidy we were. I took the minimum of things back to school, since I went home every weekend and didn't want to get too comfortable at school, while Fiona had lots of things in her area of our room. Everything of mine was tidied away in its place, but Fiona's things could be anywhere!

One summer afternoon, Fi was recording a revision tape. We had the window open as we always did when we could, for fresh air and to hear the birds. The wind must have suddenly got stronger, as one of Fi's wind chimes, which was hanging in the window, started jangling ferociously. Thinking of the recording Fi was making, I crept over to the window to close it a bit. The window was in Fi's area, so I had to carefully step over all sorts of things. I think she'd had a mad dash to find something that morning, so there was a bit more than usual on the floor. I was trying to decide where to put my foot next, when I lost my balance. I didn't want to squish anything, so I tried desperately to wobble around on one leg. The next thing I knew, I was sitting in a cardboard box full of things! I think I let out some sort of high-pitched squeak! I don't think that bit of tape was kept. It would have made us laugh too much each time we heard it.

***

Another day, in more recent years, I was at Mum's house having a cup of tea, while she did her ironing. I must have needed to go home for something, as I suddenly stood up while I was drinking the last mouthful of tea.

Before Mum could say anything, I'd turned to go around the end of the settee, but instead of that, I ended up lying across the top of the laundry basket!

My mug was still in my hand, but the slop of tea I usually leave at the bottom had slopped out onto the floor. Mum said nothing as she put the iron down, took my now-empty mug out of my hand, and went to get a cloth. She knew I still had a mouthful of tea! I managed to finish my tea before I burst out laughing. Mum not saying anything kind of made it even funnier, but she didn't want to make me laugh!

Let's just say the laundry basket was never the same after that. Several of the plastic bits were broken. I wonder why!

***

The most recent thing which comes to mind only happened a few weeks ago. I was listening to a message as I came out of my front gate and turned to go towards Mum's house. I could hear people talking, so not wanting to get in anyone's way—what with social distancing and all—I decided to get a move on. Only, as I went quickly down the pavement, I met my wheelie bin which had just been emptied! There was a huge crashing noise as I knocked it over! An empty bin makes a lot of noise! I started laughing as I picked it up. It would have to happen when there was someone about! I didn't know where they'd gone, but I turned and said in their general direction, "Guess I forgot that was there!" There was no response, so I can only hope they didn't see me at all!

The daft thing is, I always put the bin out on that side of the gate on bin day, so I'll find it and remember to take it back in again. I definitely found it that day!

14

Berta and I have been friends since we were two years old. When Berta won a weekend away at a hotel in Devon, she invited me to go with her.

So, off we went on the train. As we had to change trains in a Welsh station, we found that all the announcements are first given in Welsh, then English. It's quite scary when you first hear a voice telling you something and can't understand a word of it, but it's a relief when you realise you didn't stand a chance of understanding it, as it was a different language.

We made the most of our time in the station and learnt how to count to three in Welsh. The platform announcements were great for that! We also discovered that some place names are different in Welsh from what they are in English. Gloucester is pronounced something like "Care Goyng"! I'm not even going to go there with the spelling of it, but that's how it sounded.

Three trains and a bus later, we arrived at the hotel. It was set in lovely grounds and was only a short walk from the sea front. During the weekend Berta and I went for several walks. We enjoyed having a look around the shops and trying out the cafes, but the most memorable part of the weekend was when we decided to sit on the rocks.

The first rocks we came to on the beach were not the best for sitting on. They were either too low, or had sticking-up bits, so we made our way over and in between them until we found a good place to sit. We stayed there a while, enjoying our surroundings, before we made the decision to continue across the rocks, instead of going back the way we came. I was either wearing ballerina style shoes or flip-flops, neither of which was a problem as I'd walked over rocks in flip-flops before. Sensible shoes have never been my thing!

So off we went. We seemed to get a bit higher as we moved from rock to rock. There was no option to walk between them, we just had to step from one to another. Berta gave excellent descriptions of which way I had to stretch my foot, up, down, left, or right, as we balanced on the rocks. On and on we went. It was not a quick process, so we probably hadn't gone as far as it felt.

All of a sudden, a voice from my left called, "I wouldn't go that way if I were you." It was a man up on the walkway, who must have had a good view of the rocks. I asked him which way we should go and he started directing us.

For a while we could go side by side, but then there wasn't room for both of us. I don't know when the man realised I was blind, but he was soon giving me directions of where to put my feet, and hands, which I now needed as I couldn't balance without knowing where my feet had to go.

Up I climbed until I came to the railings, which I soon climbed through and thanked the man. It seemed I wasn't the only one who couldn't balance once I was on my own, as the man said, "Your friend's coming up on her knees!"

Berta soon joined me and after thanking the man again, we went for a well earned hot chocolate!

15

I love snow! Maybe I wouldn't be so keen if we got as much of it as some places, but because most years we get a few inches maybe once or twice—sometimes not at all—I tend to make the most of it when I can.

Berta lives fairly near me and she enjoys the snow as much as I do. If possible, she calls for me and we go out to play! Okay, we are supposed to be adults now, but there's no age limit on fun!

One year we had a good few inches, which had stuck around for a few days. Berta and I decided to call for my cousin Sophie, so the three of us could go sledging together. Sophie lives in the next village, just over the road from where I grew up. The problem was, we didn't have a sledge, so Berta solved this problem by bringing along two trays. Yes, the kind you put your dinner on to eat off your lap! I didn't have any trays to add to this, so off we went, walking the two miles to Sophie's house. We had some hot chocolate to warm us up, then it was time for the three of us to find the best sledging spots.

Sophie pointed out that we only had two trays and, although we could have just taken turns, like good big kids, Sophie decided to see what she could use from the garage. She found a potato bag! Yes, I mean those thick paper sacks with a couple of layers. I think her dad was most amused by us taking a paper potato bag, but we were sure it would be just fine.

First we went one way and sledged down a bit of a hill, but there was a scary fence a bit close by, which I wasn't keen on the idea of meeting at full speed. So Sophie suggested we go to the green near the house where I grew up. We knew from past experience that there was good sledging to be done there, so off we went. On the way, we passed by Sophie's house and abandoned one of the trays, which had broken in protest at being sat on!

We reached the green and I have to say I felt a little strange at being so close to the house I grew up in. I hadn't been that near the end of the drive since Mum and I had moved out of there to our separate houses several years before. I soon got used to it, though, and we sledged from the top green, over the narrow track which led to my old house as well as two others, to the bottom green. It wasn't quite as smooth as it used to be, as the wild boar had moved into the area and turfed it up. The second tray soon went the way of the first, so we were left with the good old spud bag!

We were doing a lot of laughing as we took turns sliding down the slopes, and we must have attracted the attention of a lady walking her dog. She came over and we all said hello and commented on the weather. She then went on to ask us if our school had been closed all week! Berta and I were in our thirties and Sophie was in her mid twenties, so I'm not sure I did a good job of keeping a straight face as I explained that we hadn't been in school for many years! I think Berta ended up sitting on the ground, she was laughing so much, and Sophie and I weren't any better! Did we really look that young, or were we just acting young! As I said at the beginning, there's no age limit on fun and I'm sticking to that! So if anyone wants to go sledging, I'll come!

16

For some reason, Mum seems to like playing with water! If she's watering the plants outside when I'm there, she usually chooses to water my feet!

If Berta and I were sitting outside, we would wonder where the spots of water were coming from, until Berta saw Mum up at her bedroom window.

It should come as no surprise, then, that she has great fun if we get snow. On one occasion, Berta had come over to my house after we'd had snow, and we decided to go for a walk in the woods when Mum took the dog. I lost count of the times Mum intentionally pinged tree branches so that Berta and I, who were walking behind her, got covered in snow.

Needless to say, another year when we got snow, Berta and I thought we'd be prepared. We decided that, as there is no age limit on fun, we would make a snowman, who would sit on the bench in my back garden. We guessed Mum would come out of her house sooner or later and put her head over the fence to speak to us, so we thought we'd have a bit of snowball ammunition ready. We made about six or eight snowballs and lined them up on the wall.

Sometime later, Mum did come out. We moved to gather our snowballs, but it was no good. We were pelted with cold snowballs, which somehow always seemed to find their way down the neck of our coats! Our pathetic amount was no match for Mum's. She had spotted our snowballs lined up on the wall, so she decided she'd go one better. Going out the front of her house, she made enough to fill a large tray and an ice cream container. Then, once her supply was complete, she came out the back and threw snowball after snowball at us. Berta and I were laughing so much we were almost on our knees!

***

On another occasion that we had snow, Martyn and Sophie came to Mum's house. I was also there, and the snow made us all act like kids again. When we heard the band coming around playing Christmas carols, Sophie and I ran outside to listen. We were by Mum's gate when a snowball landed near us. We were wondering where it came from, when another landed. The people across the road were out listening to the band too, so we wondered if they'd thrown them. Sophie suggested throwing some back, but thankfully we didn't, because we soon realised that it was Mum and Martyn up in the bedroom window aiming them at us.

I don't know what happened next, but Martyn came out and threw a few more. We got him back, then he shut the door on us! I think Sophie tried to push one through the letterbox in the door, when she suddenly turned to me and said, "Ooh, Lou! Letterbox!" as she handed me the metal flap which had fallen off the outside. Thankfully, there were brushes to stop the wind blowing through and another metal flap on the inner side of the door, but a new letterbox was required!

17

In my house, I have a good-sized cupboard under the stairs. It's amazing what I can get in there: coats on hooks on the wall, vacuum cleaner, ironing board, clothes-airer, etc. It's also a wonderful place to keep my multitudinous shoes!

When I moved here, I brought with me a bookcase I'd used for books whilst living at home with Mum. I didn't need to use it as a bookcase anymore, so I thought it would make the ideal shoe cupboard. I managed to get it into the cupboard under the stairs, but only just, as it took the whole width of the cupboard. I slid it back as far as it could go, then filled it with shoes.

This worked wonderfully, but there was a gap behind the bookcase, as the ceiling of the cupboard sloped down with the underside of the stairs. The problem with this gap was that things I put on top of the bookcase sometimes went down behind it.

One day, I decided that I'd had enough of this and decided to get down there and get everything out that had fallen down the back. I slid the bookcase forward a bit, just enough that I could climb over it and get stuff out. The top was probably about waist height, but I somehow managed to climb over and retrieve things like kitchen rolls and dusters.

Then came my next problem...getting out! How could it be that there was enough space for me to get over there, but not enough to get back over? Try as I might, I could not do it. The sloping ceiling, along with the very small space behind the bookcase, meant there wasn't enough space to sort of bounce up there. I had no phone, so I knew I had to do it somehow, or be stuck in the cupboard for who knew how long!

I couldn't turn the bookcase, and I couldn't move it much further forward, since there were things along the walls on either side of the cupboard.

I didn't know how strong the bookcase was, but decided that if it broke, it broke. I had to get out somehow. If I landed in a heap on the floor amongst shoes and a broken bookcase, so be it. At least I would be out.

So somehow, eventually, I managed to almost lie on top of the bookcase; and after a lot of manoeuvring—and the bookcase nearly tipping forward—I got my legs back over. Amazingly, it didn't break!

I decided that perhaps this hadn't been the best of ideas, so I asked my dad to use the bookcase wood to make built-in shelves right at the back of the cupboard instead. This is much more successful and gives me even more room in there.

***

That extra space has been very useful. Back in 2013, Alex wrote an audio nativity play and asked me to play the part of Mary. My first problem was where to record. The only microphone I had picked up sound from the whole room. All the rooms in my house have quite a bit of echo, because I prefer hard floors. I tried and tried to find a way of reducing the echo, until I remembered the cupboard under the stairs.

I gathered up my netbook and positioned it just outside the door. I trailed the wire inside and set the microphone down. I then gathered my keyboard and headset and went into the cupboard. To cut out as much echo as possible, I had to close the door behind me. There's no light in the cupboard, so there I was, crouching in the dark by the microphone, trying to record my lines.

You know how sometimes you try to record something and keep messing it up? Well I'd got a few scenes sorted when I came to the one I just couldn't get right. The harder I tried, the more my words came out backwards. It was the scene where Mary was waiting for Joseph to return after looking for somewhere to stay. I know it started with, "please Lord, let him come back soon." Somehow I'd made a muddle of saying that, so I went on, "because I'm shut in the cupboard and it's dark and I want to get out!" I couldn't resist sending it to Alex for a laugh.

I got to help out with some of the audio editing too, which was so much fun, as we were both learning as we went along. I especially enjoyed positioning each individual sheep to make them sound natural. I've heard enough sheep around here over the years to have an idea of how they should sound.

We had some fun trying to make it sound like someone was moving as she walked. On our first attempt, we ended up making her sound like her head wobbled. We also had fun positioning the footsteps of the men from the East. At first they were walking in perfect rhythm with one another, which didn't sound natural at all. I think we got there in the end, though, and thankfully I didn't have to do any of the audio editing in the cupboard under the stairs.

18

In 2010 I went to Thailand along with several members of my family, a friend of Mum's, and her fourteen-year-old son. We saw many interesting places while we were there and I enjoyed the experience of being in such a different country, including the foot massages you could get on the street just opposite our hotel. One day, we were eating at an outdoor restaurant, when someone noticed there was a big ball you could go in and roll somewhere. This sounded like great fun to me! It turned out that two of you had to be strapped into this ball, roll down a hill, and land on the water before unharnessing yourselves and trying to walk inside the ball to get back to land. There were only two of us brave enough to try this, Mum's friend's son and me. So they inflated the ball and positioned the steps.

I wanted to get some kind of record of this, as well as any photos the others might take, so I turned on my voice recorder and gave it to Mum to hold. I think I had to go up four or five steps before I could climb into the ball. I lay down and the person in charge fastened the straps and showed me how to release them, which I would have to do when we got onto the water. Next, it was time for Sam to get in. This meant the ball had to be turned and I was hanging upside down while they helped Sam and made sure he knew how to unfasten his straps. Then we were off, rolling down the hill. It was sort of fast and a bit bouncy! I remember laughing, and the recording from the voice recorder Mum was holding confirmed that! All you could hear as the ball rolled away from her was me going "Heeheeheeheeheeheeheeheeheeheehee". I kept that up all the way down—it hardly sounded like I took time to breathe! Mum was walking fast down the hill after us, but it took her much longer to get there.

We landed on the water with a huge swish! and the ball bobbed and bounced quite a bit. I had no idea how far we'd gone onto the lake. Sam and I unfastened our harnesses and tried to get the ball back to land. My first problem was that I didn't know where land was! Even when Sam tried to tell me, as soon as we moved I was lost again. Everything was too round. I was still laughing at this point, but not quite as much as I was trying to concentrate on what I was doing! The hardest thing was keeping away from the holes at either side of the ball, or sometimes they were at the top and bottom. Sam kept trying to warn me if I was getting near, but we couldn't get the ball to go straight. Sam was much taller than I am, so going straight was impossible! I nearly fell out of the ball, but managed to pull myself up just in time. The problem was, though, I now had a wet foot! It's very difficult to walk in a smooth, shiny ball with a wet foot. I tried to get away from that hole, but maybe I tried too hard! The next thing I knew, I slipped and fell straight out the other hole! I remember going down into the water and pushing the ball as hard as I could! I'd forgotten to ask how deep the lake was and I didn't want to get stuck under the ball. There was a massive swoosh! as I sent Sam and the ball flying away from me! I had taken in a big breath as I fell out of the ball, and thankfully I managed not to breathe in any water. I was relieved when my feet touched the bottom and I stood up to find that the water was only about four foot something deep. Water was dripping from my hair and blocking my ears, but I could just about hear Ice calling me. I think I heard Sam calling me as well, wondering where I was, but I just made my way towards where Ice's voice was coming from. I felt like a dog, shaking my head to get the water out of my ears!

I got to the bank and Ice pulled me out. Mum was just about getting to the lake by then, so you can tell how fast the ball went! I was surprised how far we'd travelled across the water. I looked like a drowned rat! I actually wore sensible clothes on that holiday, but my shorts and top were dripping! I don't think that white top ever recovered from the lake water! There were no towels, so I dripped my way back to the pickup we were using. I think Sam also got wet, as he too eventually fell out of the ball, but not as much as I did, since he fell out closer to land, where it was shallower! I think he also managed to fall out in a more civilised manner!

There were four people in the main part of the pickup, and four of us sitting in the open part in the back. That would never be allowed here, but it was a fun experience to have. There I sat, my dripping hair blowing wildly in the wind as we drove along! There are probably photos of me looking completely wild—they were all laughing, so someone must have taken one. I was a little dryer by the time we got back to the hotel, but as soon as we walked through the door, the man on reception asked with great concern, "What happened?" I think he was quite amused when we told him how I'd fallen out of the ball.

I'd love to try it again, but next time I'll be more prepared.

19

One afternoon, there were four of us in my house for a Bible study. Isn't it always the way that when you are doing something, the phone keeps ringing! I decided that the easiest thing to do was to shut the living room door, so the ringing from the hall wasn't so loud.

All was well, until it was time for everyone to leave. I went to open the living room door, but nothing happened. I turned around and calmly announced to the other three, "I'm afraid my door won't open, but don't worry, you can go out the back way."

Denise left, while the other three of us tried and tried the door. It just wouldn't open. Janet had left her shoes in the hallway, so Dot and I went out the back of my house and around to the front. I will just add here that you can't get from the front to the back of my house without going out through my back gate, down past three other houses, around the end, then up the road at the front, passing the same three houses, before you get to my front gate. I did then have a panic that I'd locked the front door, but thankfully I hadn't. I tried the living room door from the other side, but there was still no movement. I collected Janet's shoes and set off around to the back again. Now there were just two of us.

I phoned Mum to see if she had any ideas, but she said she couldn't do anything as she had a colour on her hair. I phoned Dad, who said he was cooking tea for himself and Mandy, but he could probably come the next day. So I gave up there.

I had several wonderful ideas—such as, I wonder if I could take the hinges off, since they are only pins, but that seemed complicated. I didn't know whether to burst into tears, or laughter! I think I did both! I got my screw drivers out, but I'd never seen the inside of a door handle, so I wasn't sure if I'd make things worse by taking it off. So I phoned my friends Ruth and Graham, who live up the road. In no time at all, Graham came down. First of all we communicated through the door as he took the handle off on the hallway side. There was no movement, so he came around the back and took off the handle on the living room side. It was then that he asked if I had a piece of wire. I tried desperately to think of what I might have, wondering if I still had wire from my jewellery-making days, but I didn't know. Janet had the brilliant suggestion of a circular knitting needle. I could put my hands on one of those straightaway. The end was snipped off and the wire used to pull the door catch open. We were free!

Graham also showed me how the inside of the handle had broken. He showed me how to assemble the handle, so when I bought the new one, I fitted it myself!

***

There's something satisfying about being able to fix something. Once I was living alone, I insisted on learning certain things, like how to bleed air out of radiators and how to change a tap washer. I remember my cousin Martyn teaching me about the inside of a tap, which came in very useful when it began to drip, meaning I needed a new washer. I wasn't sure exactly what I needed, so I took the tap apart and took its insides into the shop with me. I don't think they were expecting me to be changing the washer myself, but I insisted I was. They sold me the bit I needed, then came chasing after me as I left the shop. Apparently I needed a certain tool to fit this new bit onto the tap's inners, so they offered to do it for me right there in the shop. I gratefully accepted that offer, as it would have been disappointing to have got home, only to find that I was unable to put the new bit on. It was a good thing I'd taken the inside of the tap with me. They fitted the part and I took it home and successfully reassembled the tap.

20

I love words, and I love accents. It fascinates me how you can go a few miles down the road and encounter a different accent altogether. I've also found that areas can have their own words for things, one of which I discovered the other day.

Mum said she saw someone walking up the road. They were just slummocking along. My response was, "Slummocking? Did you make that up?" Mum explained it was walking along like you really can't be bothered and its all too much effort. I'd never heard that word, so I asked my friend Ruth. She knew the word well, but we decided it's probably a "Forest" word.

Here in the Forest of Dean, the accent is quite strong and considered countrified. I remember it was a great source of amusement to others when I was in school, even though the farthest I travelled for school was an hour away. There were certain words and phrases they used to try to get me to say. I was determined I wasn't going to lose my accent for anyone and wondered how they'd cope if they spoke to someone with a really strong Forest accent. Even I have to concentrate when I'm talking to a real Forester.

I remember when Alex and Jonathan first moved here from Wales. Alex and I were on the bus on the way home from Gloucester, when the driver asked someone as she got on, "King's Yud be it?" I thought I'd better translate for Alex that he was asking if they wanted to be dropped off by the King's head.

***

Along with accents go funny sayings, which I love. I think it's a shame how a lot of the old sayings are disappearing. Accents and funny words make us unique.

Both Grandma—Mum's Mum—and Auntie Betty—Dad's sister— had interesting ways of saying things. I remember Auntie Betty getting into the car once and exclaiming in a strong Forest accent, "Caw! En it 'ottified!" Translation: "Isn't it hot!"

I think adding "ified" on the end of words is definitely a Forest thing, as I remember Grandma saying, "It looks snowified." There were many other such words.

Grandma also had a way of using the wrong word, or her version of the word. She once told us that her friend had been to the doctor's and was now on breeze blocks! I think beta blockers would be more effective!

Outside the back of Grandma and Granddad's house was the patiole.

After watching an advert for the Harvester restaurants on TV one evening, Grandma announced that she'd always wanted to go to a combine harvester for a meal.

As a small plane once flew over, she wondered if it might be someone she knew up in their microwave! I know technology is moving fast, but a microlite might be more reliable.

Back in the early nineties, I was going along in the car with Mum and Grandma one day, when Grandma announced, "There's a lot of people around here with those saucepan tellies." Mum and I were confused for a while, before we realised she meant satellite dishes!

Auntie Betty was the only person I knew at the time who called the rotary washing line a "Whirly gig"!

I've always loved funny words, and I'll probably end up using them myself, just like Grandma and Auntie Betty. Already I end up creating my own words for things, so it's only going to get worse! Grandma's response was always, "Oh well, you knew what I meant!" so that's going to be my response too.

Only the other day, I was talking to Alex about someone having a vaccination. When she asked which one, I knew I was in trouble. I said, "I can't think what it's called, you're going to laugh, but if I say Minerva?" Should she be worried that she instantly knew I meant Moderna?

21

In 2009 I became friends with Alex. During the nineties we'd been at the same school for just over half a year, and Although she was only in the year above me and the classes were very small, we never knew one another at the time. Believe it or not, I was actually so quiet when I was at that school, that people didn't always know I was there.

When Alex and I met through another friend, we soon found out that we have a lot in common. We both agree that we are now like sisters. Just as people from the same family often get confused for one another, the same happens to us. True, we are about the same height and of similar build. We both like similar clothes and have long hair, but there the similarity in our looks ends. Alex has straight hair, whereas mine is bouncy. The colour is also quite different.

I've lived in this area all my life, while Alex and her husband Jonathan moved here in 2012. I once went to an event with some friends and was asked by someone I'd never met before how my husband was. I explained that I don't have a husband and that he was probably thinking I was Alex, but he insisted he knew my husband and had seen him a few weeks ago. I tried again, then gave up. It took someone else to convince him that I wasn't who he thought I was.

Another lady gave me back my umbrella. I was quite confused by this and explained that it couldn't be mine. She insisted my husband had lent it to her, from my car. At that point I gave up and decided I'd just give it back to Alex and Jonathan myself.

When I visit Alex's mother, I expect to be called Alex. At a coffee morning it was interesting to see how many people thought I was her. Some were observant, as I heard comments like, "It's not Alex," or, "the hair's the wrong colour." Quite a few people know me in that area now, but I think I got called Alex about seven times that day.

We probably confuse people too: if we have been asked to sing together, we dress the same whenever possible. People have often asked if we are twins, but now that's half the fun of it. No one seems to notice that one talks with a Welsh accent, while the other has an English accent.

You would think that as we get on the bus to go into Gloucester shopping in two completely different places, people wouldn't be so confused. That isn't so. We have both been asked our names several times, but the best was the day a lady on the bus asked me, "What is your name?" I told her I was Lou, to which she replied, "Oh yes, I knew it was something." I found it difficult to keep a straight face as I felt relieved to discover that she at least knew I had a name!

There are times, though, especially on the bus, that you just don't bother correcting them when they call you by the wrong name. One morning I got on the bus and a lady near the front said, "Morning Alex." I knew I'd told her I was Lou many times, so I just said, "morning!" Then the lady behind her said, "morning Lou," to which I replied, "Morning." I then saw the funny side: if there were people on the bus who weren't usually there, they might think I didn't know my own name!

One day when we were shopping together, one of the assistants asked, "Are you sisters, or what?" Neither of us liked the sound of the "Or what," so both said at the same time that we were sisters. If I go into that shop alone, I'm always asked where my sister is.

Alex and I often laugh about people muddling us up. You never know, it might come in useful one day, although I'm not quite sure how!

22

Neither Alex nor I like Halloween, so one year, when Alex was staying with me for the weekend while she was still living in Wales, we thought we would pretend we were not in. The house was in darkness, apart from the small light in the kitchen above the cooker.

We wanted to do something nice, so we decided to make a chocolate cake. We were about halfway through measuring the ingredients, using the talking kitchen scales, when we heard my gate open. We stood as still as we could, trying not to laugh as the doorbell rang and we heard voices outside. I knew they would only wait a minute or so before moving on.

All was quiet while they waited for someone to answer the door, until my kitchen scales suddenly announced "Zero" in a very loud male voice!

We were practically on our knees laughing while still trying not to make a sound. I don't know if those at the door heard us, or the scales, but they soon left and we got on with the important task of making chocolate cake!

23

When Alex and Jonathan moved from Wales to the Forest of Dean, it was so good to have them only living about 2 miles down the road. It meant I got to see them often and we could all go for walks together. They could call in for a cup of tea, also Alex and I could go shopping together.

One afternoon, I was in my house when the doorbell rang. I knew Alex and Jonathan had been for a walk that afternoon and I wondered if it might be them calling in for a cup of tea. After all, the ring on the doorbell was just how Jonathan did it, a couple of quick presses which gave rapid ding dongs.

I opened the door and said hello. The accent was definitely Welsh, sort of a bit exaggerated Welsh I thought, as the man at the door asked if I was interested in new windows. I was laughing as I replied, "Nah, you're okay thanks".

I was still laughing, wondering how long he could keep it up as he asked about conservatories. "I think I'll give them a miss," I said while still laughing. I was impressed he'd kept a straight face.

Then I saw it. The thing in his hand that was light in colour and probably paper. I then realised that Alex was nowhere around either. She couldn't keep a straight face for that long. It wasn't Jonathan at all! It was a genuine window salesman! I dread to think what he thought of my laughing at him, but I didn't like to admit to my confuddlement. He was on his way out through the gate by then and if I had tried to explain, he might have tried again to sell me windows which I didn't want!

***

I've always enjoyed visiting Alex's family in Wales. I have to say, though, that each time I arrived, it used to take the first afternoon to sort of tune in to her dad Jeff's accent and understand him. Jeff also had some of his own words for certain things. One day I got off the train on a damp wet afternoon. Alex was already there and she and her mother were waiting in the car. After saying hello, the first thing Jeff said to me was, "This is the kind of weather that gives you arthuritis, rheumatism and colds!" It was always "arthuritis" and I've heard several people in my family call it the same thing. Alex and I had a smile at the idea of "Arthuritis, rheumatism and colds", but guess who ended up with a cold a couple of days later? Yes, me. That's what I got for laughing.

***

When in the car with Jonathan, he often mentions idiots on the road, but because of how he says it, it sounds like "I-juts" with it almost sounding like there's a "y" in there, "i-jyuts". It must have been just after one of those occasions when Alex's brother came round and was talking to Alex and me. He sort of stretched, then said, "I suppose I'd better go and meet Jut". Again, it sounded like there was a "y" in there. Without really thinking, I opened my mouth and said, "Is that short for ijut?" Thankfully, he laughed and said that it was short for Justin. He didn't let me forget it though: when his phone rang, he said before he answered, "It's ijut!"

24

Alex and I always find something to laugh about when we go to Gloucester on the bus. I like to say good morning to people who are walking up or down the road while I'm standing at the bus stop. When I say the bus stop, there's nothing actually there, you just stand on the side of the road. There's no pavement, just a low bank going up behind you, and sometimes a mini river running down the edge of the road if we've had a lot of rain.

Not many people walk up and down the road, but I've had a few hilarious conversations with people passing by. One morning I said good morning when I heard footsteps coming along. I don't remember exactly, but maybe it was windy and I couldn't hear properly; Then again, it might have been completely quiet. After saying good morning and not receiving a reply, I suddenly realised I'd just said good morning to a sheep! They wander freely around here and I realised that there were a group of them making their way down the road.

I had a job to keep a straight face when I realised what I'd done, but I didn't want to stand there laughing seemingly at nothing, as anyone driving past would think I was daft for sure. I think eventually the sheep bahed in reply, before continuing its way down the middle of the road.

***

Some shops are easier to identify and find than others. One day there were some people standing in the way, preventing us from identifying the shop doorway. I confidently asked, "Excuse me, which shop is this?" and was told by a man who sounded quite bored, "It's a cash point." They weren't standing in a doorway after all.

***

Most people we meet are extremely helpful, even when they would have a good excuse not to be. We experienced this once when going into a shop to collect a catalog. I knew they were somewhere near the door, so I asked a person standing by the stands of larger fixed catalogs—where you can also check product availability—"Could you tell me where the catalogs are, please?"

He sort of went "Uh..." and handed me a tiny piece of paper used to write your order number on.

I then realised that he didn't speak English. Maybe I should have taken the paper and thanked him, but he seemed keen to help, so I tried to explain, demonstrating the size with my hands, "Thank you, I meant the book."

Suddenly he knew what I was talking about. He turned and retrieved a catalog and handed it to me saying, "Big book! Very heavy!"

I really appreciated that, despite the language barrier, he did his best to help.

***

We encountered similar language issues in another shop. I know now that I had gone into the clothes shop next door to the one I'd intended to visit. When I asked if they had any cardigans, there was a pause before the man replied, "We don't sell cardigans, we only sell clothes."

I did try demonstrating and explaining what a cardigan was, but failed miserably!

***

We now have a new bus station in which the different stands are easy to find, with tactile paths leading to each one. In contrast to this, the old bus station was not easy at all. Between avoiding the pigeons and bus queues snaking all over the place, it was really quite difficult to find where to go.

One day Alex and I got back to the bus station and were looking for the place from which our bus would leave. We were trying to find someone to ask, when Alex suddenly moved forward saying, "Excuse me." I could make out the object she was heading towards and couldn't keep a straight face as I said, "That's a bin!" I think we were both still laughing about that one by the time we found our bus.

***

Speaking of the bus, I had a very strange experience one day when I was getting off. We were late back to the bus, so were seated quite a way down toward the back. When we stopped where I get off, I got up and tried to go as quickly as I could down the aisle. It's actually a coach rather than a service bus, so I think the aisle is narrower. I was trying not to hit everyone I passed with my bags, but my cane, which was in front of me, kept getting stuck, stopping me abruptly. I wondered what kind of yuckiness was on the end of my cane and tried holding it a bit higher, so it wouldn't get stuck and I could get off more quickly.

Still it kept getting stuck. I was feeling quite self-conscious by this point. Even though I was able to get it unstuck fairly easily, it felt like I was taking forever to get off the bus.

I eventually did get off and made my way down the road towards home. Still my cane was getting stuck, but not as much now. Once I got into the house, I bravely investigated the end of my cane. It turns out I had a really long piece of nylon thread wrapped around the end. It was getting stuck because I kept standing on the thread!

25

I wonder how many funny looks Alex and I get as we make our way around town, as we are often laughing about something or other. People in the shops are generally quite helpful when we ask them to assist us in finding different products. Some of them in the clothes shops even get to know the kind of colours and styles we like.

There is one lady in a particular shop who remembers Alex for a hilarious reason. We got a few other things in there with her assistance before Alex announced, "My husband needs a plunger."

Let's just say the assistant and I burst out laughing! I knew that there was a problem in the bathroom and that Jonathan had asked Alex to get a plunger, but it really did sound as if Jonathan needed it personally. From then on, Alex was remembered by that assistant for the plunger incident, even years later.

***

There was a particular café we used to like. Unfortunately it's now closed, but it did the best hot chocolate, along with really good cake! There was a man who worked there who was always really friendly and helpful to us, but when we heard someone giving him instructions one day, it sounded as though he'd rather be anywhere else but there. However, it was that day that we heard him being called Ben.

I think it was the same day when we went up the stairs to the top floor, where the little rooms were located, that we somehow ended up opening the wrong door and nearly went into a funny room we hadn't known existed. I think it was Alex who named it "Ben's den". It smelt of chocolate, so we thought it was probably a store room. We were surprised it wasn't locked, as Anyone could have gone in there and had a wonderful chocolaty feast, not that it was particularly busy in the café. The thing is, for some reason, "Ben's den" intrigued us! So, before the café closed, when Jonathan also came into town one day, I sat there supposedly innocently drinking my hot chocolate, while Alex and Jonathan paid a visit upstairs, where Alex convinced Jonathan to open the door of "Ben's den" a crack. He was able to confirm that it was indeed a storeroom.

***

It's always good to spend time with friends and one day, our friend Sarah came to meet us in Gloucester. So the three of us could chat as we went around, we all linked arms, with Sarah in the middle. Our canes were almost synchronised as they swished from side to side. We were probably quite hard to miss, but it was the comment by a man as the three of us descended a flight of stairs which made us smile. I'm not really sure the best way to describe how he sounded, a bit surprised, along with a trace of amusement I think, as he exclaimed, "You don't see that very often!"

***

Alex and I have often met our friend Ines in town. We always enjoy a good look around the clothes shops, as well as visiting the cafés. We went into one shop and made our way to the counter to ask for assistance. Ines was standing a little further away, while Alex and I had our arms linked. A very enthusiastic lady came towards us. We all thought she worked there, since she asked what we needed. Never being sure who is staff and who is a customer, I took my usual safe approach as I explained that we were looking for a member of staff to help us find a few things.

I didn't know what to say as she moved behind me, put her hands on either side of my waist and announced, "I'll just place you over here." With that, she moved me backwards and to the side. As she went to tell the staff, who had probably already seen us and were arranging for someone to help us, I turned to Alex and Ines and said, "I think I've just been placed!" I half expected her to sit me on a shelf or something. She probably would have tried if there had been an empty one. I was so surprised, I didn't know what to say to her, but we definitely saw the funny side. We usually do move somewhere out of the way once someone knows we are looking for help, but she didn't give us the chance.

***

Finding the queue can be quite difficult in some shops. There can be shelves in random places, certain ways to go in and out, meaning sometimes we just end up in the wrong place! We've got hooked up on jewellery stands, with their hooks which seem to reach out and grab you. I've nearly apologised to mirrors on many occasions, and getting lost has also been quite useful at times, as we have found nice clothes to buy. After all, if we are among the clothes, we may as well have a good look at them. Alex and I have quite a good pair of eyes between us, she can see the colours, while I can see if there is a pattern and whether it's delicate, or big and bold.

One day we got lost among stands while looking for the counter to ask for help. I was quite relieved when I saw someone just standing there, not looking through racks, so I asked, "Excuse me, is this the queue?"

Without even turning, he muttered grumpily, "Does it look like a queue?" I wasn't really sure how to answer, but before I thought too much about it, I heard myself say calmly, "I don't know."

At that point he turned around and looked at us. I would have loved to have seen his face when he saw our white canes! He couldn't get his words out fast enough as he apologised and took us to where the queue actually was. I don't think we did too well at hiding our laughter after he'd left us in the right place. I'm guessing he was probably waiting for someone, and a clothes shop was the last place he wanted to be.

26

On a summer evening, there's nothing quite like going to get take-away, then sitting somewhere nice to eat it outside. Alex, Berta, and I had decided that we would go to Lydney, get burgers, then sit in the park to eat them.

I don't remember what time we had decided to go, but let's just say that Berta was running on "Berta time" that day. We ended up going much later than planned, but as it happened, it worked to our advantage.

Berta drove to Lydney, we got our burgers, then took them to the park. We found a nice bench where we could enjoy them while listening to a fountain. There were some teenagers playing ball, which was quite entertaining to observe, but apart from them, the park was empty.

I think that while we ate, we agreed how nice it would be to be children again and play on the swings. When we'd finished, Berta informed us that the swings were empty. There was no reason why the three of us couldn't have a go.

We were all in our mid thirties at the time, but we didn't hesitate and the three of us were soon swinging happily, Alex and I both wearing long skirts, while I was also wearing my usual flip-flops! Not at all the right kind of clothing for playing in the park! We discovered that each of the three swings we were using had a squeak, each on a different note. So of course we had to try to get them to squeak in time and play a tune. Why should children have all the fun? There's something freeing about swinging as high as you can, your hair flying out behind you. I think we were all relieved that no children came along wanting to use the swings.

After we left the swings, Berta informed us that there was a running track. Berta is a runner; in fact, she has competed in several marathons. I don't know who suggested that the three of us should have a race, but it was obvious from the start that neither Alex nor I would win. Berta lined us up, showing Alex and me which direction we were to run in, then off we went. I think Alex and I were both afraid of running into each other—well that's our excuse anyway—as Alex went one way off course, and I went in the opposite direction. We were all laughing so much that Alex had to stop running! I think we eventually joined Berta at the finish, which wasn't actually that far away, then made our way to some exercise equipment which had been installed.

This brought even more hilarity, as Berta tried to explain to us what we had to do on each piece of equipment. We each tried out the different things with much laughter, as you can imagine.

By this time, it was practically dark. We were having so much fun we'd lost all sense of time. When we went to leave the park, we found the gate closed and locked! Thankfully, Berta knew another way out, but we did feel like naughty children getting locked in the park. If anyone were to ask if we would do it all again, I could guarantee the answer from each one of us would definitely be yes!

27

I think the idea is that once you reach a certain age, you become more sensible. I can do sensible, but why do it all the time? As I said before, why should children, or those who have children, have all the fun?

I think the camping experiences Alex and I have had all started because Mum bought a gazebo. She wanted to try it out and, for some reason, it went up in my garden. I'm glad it did. This was at the time when Alex was still living in Wales and it just happened that the gazebo experiment occurred when she was visiting for a few days. It was a hot day and we spent all afternoon lying under the gazebo, where we were not in direct sun. We decided it would be fun to sleep out there overnight, so we did. The gazebo has three removable sides, so we put those on and got cushions and sleeping bags. We didn't have much choice in which way we should face, as at that time, my garden was on a slope.

There are all sorts of noises to be heard outside at night, from owls, which I love to hear but Alex doesn't, foxes out in the woods, or sheep which may be wandering up and down the road at the front of the house. I don't think we've heard any wild boar out in the woods at the back of this group of houses yet, but I have heard them from inside the house when my window was open. You also hear people coming and going at all times, along with the church clock a mile or so away as the crow flies. It's amazing how sound travels differently at night. The air sounds so much clearer.

On this particular night, we heard something we've never heard before, or since. It was probably about two-something and a noise made us both alert. There was something in Mum's garden, moving around on the gravel. We heard it go to the pond and drink, all the while making funny little grunty noises. We really had no idea what it was. It then made its way out under the wooden gate. There was a sort of scratchy rubbing sound and I knew instantly that it must be a hedgehog and the sound was its spikes on the underside of the gate. I've never heard one since, but it was lovely to hear it even just the once.

There's nothing quite like hearing the dawn chorus. Just before the sky begins to lighten, the temperature drops lower. Then we listen out for the first bird, which usually seems to be a blackbird. Gradually, you hear the woods come to life with bird song. You can't see the sunrise from the back of my house, but you feel the air warming up.

We decided we'd enjoyed our night under the gazebo so much that we'd do it again. By the next time, I had a level patio, which was quite different from the sloping grass. Now we could face in whichever direction we chose. It was another warm night when we decided it was time for "Camp Gazebo", as we'd named it. We heard all sorts of noises, including one of the neighbours singing, before we fell asleep. However, I woke up when Alex suddenly sat upright, turned around to face the side of the gazebo behind us, and said in a ferocious sounding whisper, "Boing!" As you can imagine, I fell about laughing and asked what was wrong. She thought an animal or something was trying to get in and wanted to frighten it off, but it was, in fact, the side of the gazebo blowing slightly in the wind and moving over the slabs, making a sort of scratchy sound. I did wonder if "Boing" would have done the job if it had been an animal, but it made us both laugh.

***

One year it was too cold to sleep out when we'd intended to, so we slept on the living room floor. The problem here was my noisy clock, which seemed to tick more and more ferociously as the night went on.

Another time it wasn't quite warm enough to be outside, so we decided to sleep on stripy lounger chairs in my garage. It's actually been turned into a room and the main up-and-over door is blocked off, so there's just the side door into my garden, which we left open. Here, the thing which kept making us jump was the freezer clicking on and being really noisy for a while, before going back off with a really loud clonk!

Some years we haven't had the gazebo up. Once we decided to sleep outside with one of us on the wooden swing and the other on a zero-gravity chair I had for a while. This was not successful. For starters, the swing isn't long enough to lie out straight on and there's only so long you can curl your legs up. How is it that when you can't straighten them, you want to! The second problem was the zero-gravity chair. You only had to move a fraction and it sat you back up again. Neither of us were able to keep it in the lying-down position. So we did the only thing we could do. We took the cushions off the swing, put them on the patio along with whatever we were sleeping under, and slept there. The ground was a bit hard, as we usually had more cushions to lie on, but at least we got to sleep out there and enjoy the birds singing in the morning.

There is one thing which has to be done when camping out and waking up to listen to the dawn chorus: you have to eat something in the middle of the night, or very early in the morning—better still, both! We've discovered that it's impossible to open a bag of crisps quietly, even if you hide them under a blanket. It's even more difficult to eat them quietly!

***

We once slept in the conservatory at Alex's parents' house. It was getting near time to hear the first bird and we decided to creep outside and find out what we could hear. We obviously didn't do too well in the creeping department though, especially when Alex kicked a watering can! Her mother soon came down to ask what we were doing.

We have also slept in my conservatory. It's not very big, so there's a bit of furniture-moving to be done, but it works well, especially if it's not too warm outside. One time, Alex was going to sleep on the folding sun lounger bed. It's not very high off the floor, but folds completely flat. I can never sleep on it though, as you only have to move a fraction and it squeaks. I turn over six hundred and two times each night, and that's before I go to sleep. The one time I tried sleeping on it, I woke myself up each time I turned over. I abandoned it after an hour or so. On this occasion, I was making my way into the conservatory, where Alex was just getting into bed, when there was a sort of crash and she burst out laughing. She'd sat too far towards the head end of the bed and it collapsed!

***

Last year we decided to do "Camp Stripes". This was basically us sleeping on the stripy loungers on my patio. They are the kind where you lift the arms to enable you to lie back. They are quite comfortable, but they don't leave much room for turning over. There is now a shade covering the back of the street light just outside my fence, which is lovely, since the garden is now much darker. I lay there looking up into the sky, trying to see stars. I spotted one or two, but I can live in hope of the light going out for a while so I can see a few more! We had the usual crisps and no doubt chocolate too, then settled down to try to sleep. I think it was as we were getting ready to hear the first bird that Alex told me she'd had a visitor. A bug had tried to get into her ear, so she'd flicked it away!

You never know what's going to happen when you camp out, but that's half the fun of it! I will also say that most times Alex stays over here, we are very civilised and sleep in the house! I even call the small spare room "Alex's room"!

28

It seems that yarn, or wool as we tend to call it, especially white wool for some reason, can get us into trouble.

One day my friend Janet came to visit. I'm not sure why, but I was knitting as we sat chatting. When my phone rang, I got up to answer it, carefully taking my knitting with me, so I wouldn't drop any stitches. The only problem was that when I returned to the settee with the phone, I somehow turned around and ended up with the wool wrapped around me. I didn't realise what had happened at first, so I turned again to see what I was hooked up on, therefore tying myself up in white wool!

Let's just say that Janet was laughing so much that she went out of the room, while I tried to finish my phone conversation while trying not to laugh too much at being tied in knots! I then had the task of untying myself; thankfully, this didn't take too long once I finally worked out which way I'd turned!

**

Another day, Alex, Berta, and I went to Gloucester together on the bus. I think Alex must have stayed at my house overnight, since she had her knitting with her. I didn't give that much thought until we were in a shop and Alex announced that she couldn't move her arms! Somehow, her wool had snaked its way out of one bag and attached itself to her other bag. It had crossed in front of her, as she had a bag on each shoulder!

You can imagine the hilarity in the middle of the shop, as Berta and I tried to untangle Alex and get the white wool free from the zip, in which it was securely attached! We finally got it back under control and into the bag where it should have stayed all along!

***

Someone once gave me a cone of wool. I used quite a bit, then decided the cone was looking a bit sorry for itself. I thought the best thing to do was to re roll the wool into a ball. I rolled and rolled, and was surprised at how much was actually on the cone. It got to the size of a tennis ball...and kept growing. It probably got to three times the size of a tennis ball by the time I'd finished rolling.

I've no idea why it wasn't in a bag, and I guess I must have had the knitting needles and the completed work in my hands as Mum and I travelled home in her car.

She pulled up the slope into her driveway and I opened the door to get out, squishing between the car door and the fence. Somehow, my nice spherical ball of off-white wool bounced out of my hand and...you guessed it, rolled down her drive.

I think I squeaked, "Oh no! My wool's gone! Can you catch it?" So Mum took off after it. She chased it down the road and past several houses. She caught it just before it rolled under a parked car. I think she said, "If it had gone under the car, it would have stayed there!"

Amazingly, it was still clean! Even more amazingly, it hadn't unrolled at all!

29

I've never liked thunder. It doesn't bother me as much as it used to, unless it comes at night when there's no one else in the house. I remember many thunderstorms when I was a child and I'm sure they used to last for hours. At night I Used to slide right down under the covers, which used to get very warm. However I'd have to keep poking my head out every couple of minutes, just to make sure everything was okay. One of the really scary storms came when I was about ten. Mum and I were in the house on our own, and I got into bed with her. Amid all the flashing and banging, the cordless phone, which was right by me on the cabinet next to the bed, made a sort of dinging noise. I was more concerned about the thunder at the time, but after that, the phone wouldn't work. When someone looked at it, they told us it had been struck by lightning! I'm not quite sure how, but it was kind of scary, especially considering how close to me it had been. I'd been told stories about my Nan getting an electric shock while speaking on the phone during a thunderstorm, and I'd also heard about a phone socket being blown completely off the wall. I stayed well away from phones during storms after that.

***

One evening when I was about seventeen, I'd been to play skittles as was usual on a Thursday. Grandma was also on the skittles team—I think the two of us used to compete for the lowest score —and Mum also played when she wasn't working evenings or nights. On this occasion she was working nights. As we came outside, I heard thunder in the distance. I had no desire to go home and spend the night alone with the thunder, in a house where I couldn't easily get to a neighbour for help, so I announced to Grandma, "I'm sleeping at your house tonight." I think she was relieved, as she never liked thunder either. We were dropped off at her house, by which time the thunder was getting nearer. Grandma got candles and matches ready; and it was a good thing she had, because within less than five minutes, there was a huge crash of thunder and the electric went off. Grandma made us a cup of tea, using a saucepan on the gas hob, and there we sat, neither of us wanting to go to bed while it was thundering. For some reason, whenever the thunder rumbled, it vibrated through the wooden front door and made the door knocker rattle! It was like something from a scary film I'd never want to watch!

Eventually, the thunder rolled away, and we could go to bed. Where did I sleep? Not in either of the spare bedrooms, but on the floor of Grandma's room, of course! Did I really just admit to that? I've since had to get used to being alone in a thunderstorm, so I no longer invite myself to sleep at someone's house when there's a storm on its way!

***

One late afternoon, Alex and I were sitting in the conservatory at her parents' house, when the air seemed to suddenly change. I said, "I don't know, but does it feel like thunder to you?" Alex had no sooner agreed when the first loud rumble was heard. I've never known the air to change so suddenly just before a storm, as you usually feel it building up. I've watched the sky darken within a matter of about a minute on several occasions, but the sudden change in the atmosphere was a whole new experience.

***

It was a Monday evening, and Alex and I were covering an Internet radio show for someone. It was one of those really hot, humid days and we just knew that thunder was on the menu! We were doing the show off Alex's laptop in my house, where it was so hot that we had the doors open to the outside. I've never heard the swifts make so much noise and they kept it up all through the show. Thankfully, people enjoyed hearing them. I think we were both relieved when the show ended and the thunder hadn't arrived.

We went outside at about ten o'clock to see if we could cool off at all. It was so quiet and still, and the scent of the flowers seemed extra strong. At that point, there was no fence between my garden and Mum's, as we were waiting for the new one to be put up, so Alex and I went around both gardens, trying to identify all the plants and see which were giving off the best and strongest scents. We had both gone outside barefoot and the slabs of the patios were very warm to walk on. Most people seemed to be in bed by this time, including Mum, who put her head out of her bedroom window to speak to us. We spoke to her in a whisper, then turned to go back to my place. Suddenly, Alex exclaimed in a loud whisper, "Yuck! I've stepped on something squidgy!" I laughed, of course, and said it was probably a slug! Alex walked with the front of her foot up in the air, back into the house to wash her foot! Sure enough, Mum saw the squished slug on the patio the next day.

We knew thunder was imminent as we went to bed a while later.

I know it takes Alex longer than me to go to sleep, so I asked her to let me know if she heard thunder, as I didn't want to be woken up by it. Alex dislikes thunder as much as I do, so we knew we'd end up getting up when it came. I'd hardly dropped off to sleep when I heard her call across the landing that it was thundering. It didn't take long for it to get close and I've never seen so much lightning! By this time we were down in the living room, Alex with her hand over her eyes so she wouldn't see the lightning. I'm completely opposite and need to see it to know what's happening. So I sat there, sharing a commentary on the lightning. I think there was sheet and fork lightning, sometimes there were three or four flashes together. The thunder got really loud and went on for ages! I don't think we had much sleep, but I was relieved that I wasn't in the house on my own. As I said, I've had several thunderstorms at night in the fifteen years I've lived here and I have got used to being on my own, but I always go downstairs, just in case I have to escape! A good imagination can be very useful for some things, but not others!

***

Every year Pat from Chapel has an open day. There's always good food to be had, various things to buy, and it's always a good chance to see people and catch up for a chat. Alex and I have been a few times, but often with someone else. I don't know why, but there was no one to go with this time, but I had a plan. I knew roughly where Pat's house was; however, around here you don't get straight streets with evenly spaced houses and obvious drives, so I decided to phone Pat's house and ask her to ask someone to keep an eye out for us, as we were on our way. Pat's house is set back off the road and you have to first find the drive, then find some steps and go down them. This is not a problem if you can find the steps, but I thought that if someone could meet us at the end of the drive, we would be fine. I don't think I explained myself properly though. As we made our way along the road past Chapel, we heard the first rumbles of thunder in the distance. We weren't too worried, since we knew we'd be there in a few minutes. We picked up speed as the sky darkened and the thunder got nearer. I thought we were getting near Pat's house but no one was there, so I thought perhaps we hadn't gone far enough. The thunder was rumbling ever nearer as I confessed to Alex, "I know we've gone too far now because we're too close to the main road." The wind was picking up as we turned back and the thunder increased in volume. We knew the rain would be there at any moment. I tried listening for the sound coming from the house, but we couldn't hear anything other than thunder. It felt like we were in some scary scene of a book or film, lost out in the thunderstorm! We were both laughing, but we were both keen to get to our destination. I thought about running back home instead, but that would have taken far too long. Back and forth we went, until the postman appeared! He knew us, and spoke to us as he stopped to deliver letters to someone. I didn't hesitate to ask him where Pat's house was, and thankfully he led us right to the drive. Still there was no one around, and the big spots of rain were just beginning to fall. I took a chance, and with both of us poking around with our canes, we found the steps and made our way down. We got inside the house just in time! The rain came down and the thunder crashed overhead!

30

I have to say it again, there's no age limit on fun! It's a good thing too, because Alex and I have done some daft things.

Years ago, I bought some adult sized space hoppers for a family barbecue. They caused much hilarity as we bounced around the orchard on them. When I moved here I couldn't part with them, so they've been deflated in their box in the back of the garage for years.

All good space hoppers need to be used, so that's exactly what Alex and I did one spring evening a few years ago. I have to say that even inflating them is good exercise when you have to use a little foot pump! I think we kept taking it in turns, since it soon makes your leg ache. Besides, I only have one pump! Eventually, we had them inflated and ready to go.

Both Alex and I spent lots of time on space hoppers when we were little, but it took a bit of time to remember how to bounce and actually move at the same time, rather than bouncing up and down on the spot! Back and forth we went across my patio! I'm surprised the neighbours didn't come to see what all the hilarity was about! I have to say, neither of us could keep up space hopping for as long as we could when we were younger!

***

I don't know why we ended up with a bag of balloons, but we did. One summer evening we decided to use some of them as water balloons. I was a bit afraid they would burst in the house as we carefully filled them from the bathroom tap, tied them, then threw them out of the bedroom window to see if they'd burst! Am I really admitting to this? We hadn't filled them too much, so some burst, while we heard another just land and bounce about.

Alex then said, "I wonder what would happen if we threw one out without tying it up?" I had an idea of what would happen, but said, "Try it!" Alex positioned herself by the open window and held the balloon out with the water filled part dangling below the neck. She let it go and my prediction, which I'd kept to myself, happened. Water shot up in the air like a fountain, getting Alex and the windowsill a bit wet, before the balloon fell to the patio below.

The following day when Jonathan came to get Alex, we again had fun with water balloons. I remember Jonathan running down the steps away from us, as Alex prepared to launch a water-filled balloon at the garage wall. I've seen Alex aim balloons at the wall before, so I knew that Jonathan wasn't in as safe a place as he thought he was. Sure enough, Alex's balloon went sailing to the left, hitting the wall near where Jonathan was standing!

Jonathan had called our attempts of water balloons weedy and pathetic. He was right! They were never huge and were always still very squishy! So, to the outside tap he went, where he attached a balloon. I remember hearing the water going into the balloon, on and on it went! I went to stand at the opposite end of the patio, which isn't that far away, expecting it to burst and soak us at any moment. At last Jonathan was happy he'd filled the balloon to capacity. He then had the task of tying it. I have to say I was still expecting it to burst at any moment! Finally it was tied.

I carefully inspected it with arms outstretched. It was huge! I would never blow a balloon up that big, let alone fill it with water! That thing was going to burst in style!

I made sure the door was shut into the house, while Jonathan went to the lower patio. Alex and I stood against the fence, while Jonathan launched his water balloon up to where we were standing. It hit the wall of the house and burst in style, soaking us and making a huge puddle, which seemed to cover most of the patio! That's how to really do water balloons!

***

A couple of years later, we became a little more civilised! It was on Alex's birthday that we inflated five light-up balloons. We'd never seen them before, so wanted to see what they were like. The tiny bulb in the bottom fills the whole balloon with light. They were each a different colour—blue, green, red, white and yellow. I love how a tiny bulb can give off so much light.

We wondered where we could hang them, and decided the washing line would be best. Out into my back garden we went, and that's where we put them to light up the night sky. It was relaxing to watch them gently moving back and forth in the breeze.

We've had more light-up balloons since then. There's something about them that makes them always seem so cheerful. Last year on the day which falls exactly between Alex's and my birthdays, we had light-up balloons hanging all around my conservatory.

31

I've always enjoyed travelling by train. Over the last several years, I've used them many times to travel to and from Wales, often on my own, but sometimes with Alex.

It can be quite entertaining to hear random bits of conversation while you sit there. Alex and I have both made the same observation: The further you get into Wales, the greater the chances are that you'll hear someone talking about pie and chips!

Many trains seem to have announcements to alert you to which stop you are arriving at, but not those on the line we use. Very rarely do we hear any kind of announcement. This is usually fine, since we can count the stops. We also know the time our train is due to arrive at the station at which we need to get off. There are now more apps available to tell you your location, but before I had these, I found the weather app very useful as that gave me my location.

One evening, Alex and I were travelling back from Wales together. It was about nine o'clock and the train was very quiet. I'm not sure if there were signalling problems or something, as we seemed to be stopping a lot more than usual. It was also one of the times when the guard didn't come to check our tickets, so there was no one to ask where we were.

There are two types of trains we get on that line; usually they are very open, with the only doors being those you use to get on and off the train. But on this occasion it was what Alex and I call the "posh trains", since they have carpet on the floor and doors at the end of the carriages too. These doors can be a nightmare, because it seems to me the buttons are never in the same place. Once you press the button, the doors open for so many seconds, before sliding themselves closed again.

By the time the train had stopped and started several times, then hung around for several minutes somewhere near Lydney station, Alex and I were totally confused as to where we were. We knew we were in Lydney, but were we at the station? There aren't many lights at the station, which only small, with two platforms and no buildings or anything, so there was nothing to let us know. There also didn't seem to be anyone sitting nearby on the train to ask, apart from someone with loud music coming through headphones, whose attention I had no idea how to attract.

I stood up and gathered my things. I was looking for the button, still not sure if we were actually in the station, when I heard the hiss which indicated the outer doors had been released. I turned to Alex who was still in our seat, which was one of the nearest to the doors and said, "This is it."

I found the button and the inner doors opened. Thinking Alex was just behind me I took the few steps to the outer doors and somehow found that button. I stepped down off the train, then turned to see where Alex was. She was not behind me. Aware that the train wouldn't be long in moving off out of the station, I called urgently, "Alex? Where are you?" It was at that moment I heard her exclaim three words loudly: the first rhyming with sit, the second rhyming with muddy, and the third word was doors— and Alex didn't usually swear!

I knew what had happened, as I'd had a similar experience before. The inner doors had begun to close on her and her bags as she was going through them, and she was stuck. I didn't know whether to jump back on the train to help her find the button, since it's impossible when you are sandwiched between two doors, or stay by the outer doors to try to make sure they didn't close again, with the train going off with Alex still on it. I jumped back on and sort of stood between the outer doors, hoping they wouldn't shut and squish me between them. I didn't think the train could move off if the outer doors weren't shut, and I reasoned in that split second that someone would have to come and investigate why. I just hoped they didn't squish me too hard if they did shut!

Thankfully, I didn't have to find out, as Alex gave the inner doors a good hard push and soon joined me. We successfully got off the train without any further problem, but the doors soon closed behind us and the train moved off.

***

On another occasion that Alex and I were travelling back from Wales together, we actually had station announcements. We jumped a mile when a loud bing bong filled the air, followed by a good clear voice giving us the next station. We commented how useful that was, but soon changed our minds. Somehow the announcements were out of sync with where the train actually was. Every couple of minutes the loud bing bong would make us jump, followed by a completely inaccurate announcement as to where we were. It announced stations we'd never heard of, it announced that we were in Cardiff when we had already passed that and were in Newport. They then seemed to be trying to get the announcements caught up, but they never got them quite right. Sometimes there was no announcement at all, just the good old bing bong! I think they were still trying to synchronise the announcements with the stations by the time we got off.

32

Hammocks can cause much hilarity! My first experience of a hammock was when my friend Fiona and I went in one at her grandparents' house. It was tied between two trees and it was very relaxing just lying there, but it had a way of slowly lowering itself until it was only a few inches off the ground, which could give you quite a surprise when you went to get out of it.

***

My next experience was about ten years ago. I went with Mum to visit her friend Chris and the hammock was put up for me to use. I was really comfortable, lying there listening to the birds and looking up through the trees. I was enjoying the patterns created by the sun shining between the leaves, when all of a sudden, I found myself sitting on the ground. I didn't squeak or anything, I was too surprised to squeak! I didn't really think about what I was doing, but apparently I calmly picked up my flip-flops and stood up, just as though that kind of thing happened every day. The rope was old and had snapped. My calmness made it all the more hilarious to Mum and Chris.

***

There are no trees in my garden, which just isn't big enough, so when I had the chance of a hammock on a stand, which could go on my patio, I thought that was a much safer option. There were no ropes to break, for a start!

I had success at getting in and out of the hammock and didn't fall out once. It really was quite comfortable. However, When Berta came one afternoon and tried it out, she didn't have much success in getting into it. I don't know how many times she got in one side and came out the other! Eventually, she did manage it, but I think she was almost too afraid to move! We did a lot of laughing, I know that. I went to go to the house for something and as I had nothing on my feet, I didn't want to go around either end of the hammock frame and risk hitting my toes on the concrete flowerpots. Berta had abandoned the hammock by then and was sitting on the swing when I announced, "I'll take a shortcut!" Under the hammock I ducked, crouching low as I went. The next minute I was on my hands and knees! I had forgotten the bar which ran underneath along the length of the frame! I think it hurt more than any flowerpot might have, but of course, I still laughed!

I came to the conclusion that my patio just wasn't big enough for a hammock. I'm perfectly happy with my swing seat at the bottom of the garden. When we have the weather, it's the perfect place for my first cup of tea of the day. There's also something relaxing about sitting on the swing in the evening. Okay, maybe I could sit on the swing all day if I didn't have anything else to do. Much of this book has been written and edited while I've been sitting on the swing.

33

I've known Janet for about twenty years, during which time we've attended the same church and sang in the same choir. We have become very good friends over the years and have all sorts of conversations. We have often commented on how we can form friendships with people of all ages.

Every Thursday there is a bus which comes around the local area and takes us into Gloucester. It then returns three hours later. It can be a bit limiting having to work everything around the weekly bus, but it's just good to have it, otherwise getting to and from Gloucester isn't so straightforward.

This is the same bus Alex also gets on when she comes to Gloucester. For quite some time, the three of us had a kind of tradition. As soon as we got off the bus, we'd go into a particular café, where Janet would have coffee and a teacake, while Alex and I had tea and iced buns. Do you get the impression we like cafés? You would be correct! One hot summer's day, we had stayed in the nice café for some time before the three of us made our way out. The tables don't seem to be in nice tidy lines, so getting through them can be quite a challenge! Janet was in front, I was following, holding Janet's arm, while Alex was on my arm, making a sort of train! Like this we wove our way through the tables to the door. It's quite a heavy door and Janet commented on how awkward it was as she opened it. It was when we got outside that Janet started laughing and said, "You won't believe this, we just struggled with that door and we didn't need to at all. The whole of the front is open!" We burst out laughing.

It turns out that the windows across the front of the café slide right back and leave the whole front open, apart from the door of course! We always checked after that.

***

There are several tables and chairs outside the café, but we don't use them. This is partly because it's where people sit to smoke, and partly because of the pigeons and seagulls. We are nowhere near the sea, but the gulls must have come up the river Severn or something. We were once again leaving the café, when there seemed to be a lot of pigeons walking around in front of us. Alex and I had to laugh when Janet told them, "Move out of the way! Haven't you got enough sky space?" As I don't like birds flapping around me, I definitely wish they'd stay in their sky space!

***

One Thursday our friend Sarah was coming to meet us. She was coming by train and I knew I couldn't find the train station to meet her, especially with all the work on the new bus station which was going on at the time. I asked Janet if she would come with us, and I'm so thankful she agreed! I would never have found my way past all the diversions, and it was so noisy we couldn't even have a conversation most of the time. We made it to the train station and met Sarah, then started on our walk back into town. The diversions made the pavement really narrow to walk on and the extreme noise of the machinery made it impossible for any of us to follow with our canes. Janet was in front with Sarah on her arm. I walked behind Janet—I remember we linked little fingers to keep contact—while Alex was behind me on my arm. There was no chance of conversation as we made our way through. As we were crossing a road and could just about hear ourselves think, Janet said, "You do realise that we only have one good eye between the four of us?" All I can say is that one good eye did an excellent job!

***

One memorable occasion, Alex and I had a successful shopping trip. We had bought quite a few things, including fairly large duck egg blue laundry baskets. To make things easier while we were walking around town, we stacked the baskets together and piled everything into them. This was fine, until we realised when we were on the bus home that we needed to separate the baskets, along with the other things we'd bought, since Alex and I get off the bus in different places. We soon discovered it's very difficult to separate several bags of shopping, along with two laundry baskets, while sitting in quite a confined space. Thankfully, our friends Janet and Mary were sitting behind us, and they came to the rescue. First of all we passed several bags of shopping over the back of our seat, which they held for us while we separated the baskets. Bags went to and fro while we then separated out their contents! It would have looked quite strange to anyone who may have been watching, but we were just thankful Mary and Janet were sitting close enough to lend a hand. If we'd put the bags down on the floor, they are sure to have slid off somewhere as the bus made its way along!

34

Isn't it easy to misunderstand something or mishear something? Just before writing this section, I was scrolling through Facebook. I got quite concerned and wondered what kind of thing was happening when I heard the speech on my phone read, "Public nude survey weekend." I think I said out loud, even though there was no one else here, "What? Seriously? No!" Then I read it again. It had actually said, "Public newt survey weekend." I don't know how you survey newts, but I'm not going to worry about that. At least there was nothing dodgy going on.

***

I was somewhere in my teens when I went to a doctor's appointment at the surgery. Mum took me there and came to the desk with me when I booked in. I didn't know which doctor I was seeing, so I asked. The receptionist replied, "I'll just have a look," before walking off. Mum thanked her and went to turn away, so I whispered in some confusion, "She hasn't told us yet!"

I could tell Mum was trying not to laugh, but once we found out which doctor I was seeing and then sat down, she couldn't help but laugh as she told me what had happened. There had recently been a new doctor at the surgery who was German. When the receptionist said, "I'll just have a look," Mum heard, "Doctor Stuffaluck!" She presumed that was the name of the German doctor. Neither of us could stop laughing, and the fact that everyone else was being so serious made it even more funny!

***

For several years, I sang with a choir. I think it was only my first or second Christmas when we learnt O Holy Night. I'd never heard this before, but I liked it. Often in songs there can be a slight variation in the lyrics. This version had two verses, the second of which is not in all versions. We were travelling home one night after choir and must have been discussing the lyrics, when I asked Jane, "What is a lowly bend anyway?" the last line of the verse was "behold your king, before the lowly bend." Jane explained it meant, before the lowly, bend. I'm guessing I wasn't told about the comma when the words were dictated to me. I remember Jane saying, "Did you think it was like an s-bend or a u-bend or something?" I think I must have. I've since heard versions which say, "behold your king, before him, lowly bend", which makes much more sense to me!

***

When I was a child in primary school, assembly was my favourite part of the day, as we got to sing hymns. I didn't like reading when I was a child, probably because my Braille books were so much larger than those my sighted friends had. I also never seemed to be able to read as quickly as they did. I found it much quicker to memorise the words of the hymns. This was mostly successful, but sometimes what I heard the others singing wasn't actually what was written. I was fascinated by the idea of a "dance settee". I loved dancing and we had a settee at home, but I wasn't allowed to dance on it. I wondered what a dance settee was and wanted to try one out, after all, the hymn said, "Dance, dance, wherever you may be. I am the Lord of the dance settee"! It was quite some years later when I realised that it was actually saying, "I am the Lord of the dance, said he". I was quite disappointed there was no such thing as a dance settee.

***

I once decided to look up whether frankfurters were available from the supermarket where I do my online shopping. When I heard the speech on my phone say, "Herd of ten frankfurters", I had hilarious images of all these sausages lined up and charging about like a herd of animals. I then read it letter by letter and found it said "Herta ten frankfurters". That made so much more sense, but I can't hear that now without having images of sausages charging about a field.

***

Why are some of the best things from the bakery designed for children? Maybe when I go in and ask for gingerbread men, they think I'm buying for a child. One day, Alex and I went into a bakery in town and to my dismay, there were no gingerbread men. The lady serving said, "We do have bat biscuits, though, and they are gingerbread with chocolate on them."

I decided they would be really good. I thought that was a really sensible shape for the gingerbread biscuit with chocolate on, since the handle of the bat would probably be plain gingerbread, so you wouldn't get chocolate on your fingers.

Alex and I made our way back to the bus and I pulled out my biscuit. At first I thought it was broken, since it sort of had sticking-out bits around the edges and wasn't rounded at all. I wondered what game you would play with that kind of bat.

When I explained my confusion to Alex, she wondered if, as it was October, they might be Halloween bats. I was so disappointed. I could see straightaway that this was the case. I don't like Halloween and didn't want to buy anything to do with it. I wasn't going to let the biscuit waste though, and I have to say they are really good.

So when October comes around and the bat biscuits come into the shop, I buy them in memory of my bat confusion!

***

My stepsister Natalie and her husband Jack have two children, Tallulah and Rocco. I think Tallulah was just coming three years old when she heard Natalie say, "I'm just going to the loo." Tallulah hadn't seen me for a while and had apparently been asking about me. Not realising what Natalie meant, Tallulah exclaimed, "I want to see Auntie Lou!" Natalie then had to explain to her that she was not going to see me, but going to the toilet.

***

On Christmas Eve Alex and I have a tradition where we go to as many services as we possibly can. Once it gets dark, we go dressed in long velvet dresses. If we can't wear our best clothes at Christmas, when can we?

We couldn't go to any services in 2020, so Alex and I dressed in warm clothes and set off to sing Christmas Carols around the village and outside the houses of our friends. Everyone was feeling a bit fed up, so we decided to decorate ourselves, each with a strand of tinsel with battery-operated LED lights wrapped around it. Up and down the roads we went, singing all the way.

Mary told us we looked like Christmas trees walking down the road!

In 2019, when we could still go to services, Alex and I went to Mum's house for tea. As it was Christmas Eve, she'd just cooked a piece of beef and we were having warm beef rolls. Chris was also there and he was having tea as well. Mum made the rolls and brought them in. Alex Asked, "Could I be cheeky and have a bag of crisps, please?" Mum gave her the crisps and we all enjoyed our tea. When Chris is there, there's usually some sort of hilarity. He says all sorts of things, and you have to give as good as you get!

When we were finished, Alex got up off the settee to take her plate out. As she passed Chris, she asked, "Shall I take your plate?" Chris thanked her and handed her his plate. Alex said, "I'll do anything for my crisps!"

"Thank you!" Chris exclaimed. There was a pause before he added, "Did you say Chris, or crisps?" Alex was laughing as she said she'd actually said crisps. We were all laughing by then, as we realised Chris had thought for a moment she'd said "I'll do anything for my Chris!" Alex jokingly referred to him as "my Chris" after that.

35

I'm sure there have been many times when those I've been with had wished they could pretend they didn't know me at all! Here are just a few examples.

I love putting together the shoe boxes which go to children in disadvantaged countries. I can never decide which age group to make a box for, so I have in the past done one for each. I don't have children of my own to buy for, and I really love trying to find different things to go in the boxes, and of course, the things I get have to be worth having! One year I decided to look for a light-up flashing ball to go in one of my boxes. I was shopping with Mum and Chris, when Chris found a display of all sorts of bouncy balls. There's no point in getting any old ball, it has to be the right size, the right colour, and of course it has to bounce well! Bounce testing when buying any kind of ball is essential! Chris tried handing me one or two to bounce test. If they had been larger balls, I would have given it a go, since I stood a chance of finding them again. However, I was less sure about these balls which were only a little larger than a tennis ball. Chris bounced a few, while Mum pretended she didn't know us and went into the next aisle. Some hardly bounced at all, while others were quite good. Chris finally convinced me to bounce one and, to be honest, there's something quite satisfying about bouncing a ball. He said he'd find it if I lost it, so I took the ball and gave it a good bounce! It hit the floor, then I heard it hit a shelf. Not only did it hit the shelf and roll and bounce around noisily for a while, it hit the button of a musical toy, which immediately began playing jingly jingly music! It was really loud! Chris doesn't do anything quietly, so he burst out laughing at full volume too! What were the chances of me bouncing a ball and setting a musical toy off! Needless to say, that ball passed the bounce test and I bought it.

***

There's something about bouncy balls that always seems to get me into trouble, but this time it was Alex as well. We were in a shop with my dad when we found a basket of balls. We were looking for a pretty-coloured ball for a little girl, so we began sorting through them. There were all sorts of different colours and designs to look at. Unbeknownst to us, the basket didn't have solid sides. There were just thick stringy pieces holding the balls inside the metal frame. Once one ball bounced out, it seemed they all started on their escape to freedom! We had no idea how they were escaping at first. Within about ten seconds, four bounced out. My dad immediately began chasing after them, three in one direction and one in the other. He tried kicking them back to us, but they overshot and he had to chase them in the other direction. Soon he had all the balls back under control and we found the one we were looking for to give as a gift. I'm guessing anyone looking at security cameras would have had some entertainment!

***

I'm happy for anyone to ask me any questions they like. Whether I'll give them the kind of answer they are hoping for, though, is another thing. As I've said before, people often think Alex and I are sisters, which is fine with us, as we see one another as sisters.

It gets a bit much, though, when people in shops constantly ask me who it is I'm with if I'm not on my own or with Alex. One particular lady knows who my dad is now and assumes he has two daughters. One day, though, I couldn't resist having a bit of fun. I was with a friend, whose name I'll not mention, since she wanted to disappear into a hole in the floor when this happened and has never been in that shop with me since! We found the things we needed and went to pay. I was asked where my sister was and explained she was out for the day with her husband. I was then asked, "Who's this with you today then?" Without hesitation I replied with a laugh, "This is my other sister!" I then somehow kept a straight face until we were outside. I knew what I'd said wasn't at all believable, but really saw the funny side of it. Most people don't get asked who they are with every time they enter a shop, and while I know she was only being friendly and making conversation, I didn't feel like being questioned. My friend couldn't believe what I'd said and pointed out that she couldn't even be my mother! I don't think she'll ever go into that shop with me again!

***

Another incident happened when I was in a café with Dad and Mandy. We'd just finished our tea and whatever we'd had to eat, when someone I hadn't seen for about five or so years came over and said hello. I recognised who he was and said hello to him. I'm never afraid to ask if I'm not sure who someone is, even if you do feel a bit silly sometimes, but what I don't like is someone asking, "Do you recognise my voice?" to which I once replied, "Yes, but I can't remember who it belongs to." This time however, the man asked, "Do you know who I am?" I replied

"Yes," then asked how he and his family were. I don't like being tested and I felt he was doing just that. Why can't someone just simply say quietly it's... whoever they are. I did know who he was and hoped he would just accept that. He then asked again if I knew who he was and I said that I did. He obviously wasn't satisfied with this and asked, "So who am I then?" I don't know how I thought so quickly, but I replied, "Don't you know?" He still didn't get my point as he said, "Well yes, I know who I am, but do you?" to which I simply replied, "Yes." There was no way I was going to give in and prove that I did. If he didn't trust that I actually knew, then he would have to continue wondering whether or not I was telling the truth. He has quite an unusual way of speaking, so I was in no doubt at all. I haven't seen him since, or maybe he's seen me but hasn't dared ask me again if I know who he is.

***

The final one in this section could have been embarrassing, but thankfully I realised in time and didn't say what I thought. Alex and I were in Wales. Along with Alex's mother and several friends from her church, we went into Cardiff to a lovely Christmas concert with a choir, an orchestra, and a children's choir. It was all lovely music with meaningful words. Before the concert, we went and had lunch; then when we got to the venue, we visited the little rooms. It all seemed very posh and I was only half surprised when I saw a Christmas tree in the toilets, not far from the hand basins. I was just about to comment on this to the lady I was with, when it moved! I hadn't seen a Christmas tree at all, it was a lady in a spotty rain coat. It had a dark background with tiny light spots. It all looked very shiny, probably from the rain outside. The spots looked to me like lights on a Christmas tree! I was so relieved that I hadn't said anything out loud, but when we were a little further away, I told Merle what I thought I'd seen and how relieved I was that I hadn't commented at the time! Turning to look, she said she could see the person I was referring to! So there were no Christmas trees in the toilets after all!

36

My good friend Ruth and I usually walk to Chapel together on a Sunday morning. Although the road we take is the same each week, no two Sundays are ever the same. I never know what Ruth is likely to turn up with, as she often has items to be stored at Chapel until the next auction. We usually end up carrying them between us, or taking turns carrying them if we're dealing with something small and heavy. I've had a few strange things for us to carry myself, but one day we got to wondering what people might think when they saw us walking along the road with all kinds of random things. I must add here that we are not talking about a busy road where we have a pavement to walk alongside it, so you would be correct in thinking there wouldn't be too many people to actually see us. The road we walk along for most of the way is narrow and has no pavement, so when a car passes, usually at the narrowest part, we have to move into the side, sometimes into brambles, where we try to manoeuvre whatever we are carrying out of the road as well. Add in potholes, puddles, or what horses or sheep have left behind, and you should have a pretty accurate picture.

In a moment of madness, I wrote the following poem...

It was on a Sunday morning,
the day was sunny and bright.
As I took in the view from my window
I saw a most peculiar sight!

They were walking towards the Chapel,
A pushchair they pushed as they went,
Not a child, a teddy or doll was in sight,
I wondered, what was their intent?

I've seen them before off to Chapel
With boxes of all shapes and sizes!
With bags which looked awkward and heavy,
To watch them was full of surprises!

Table lamps, plant pots and pictures,
Stools and folding chairs!
Heaters, rugs, clothes-airers, light tubes!
Even a teddy bear!

The chimney brushes were most amusing!
They looked so awkward and tall!
But my favourite of all was the exercise ball,
I thought, they will bounce back if they fall!!!

37

On many occasions, Alex and I have met my dad in town after we've done our shopping. Instead of going home on the return version of our once-a-week bus, we go to some of the out-of-town shops with him. We then go back to his and Mandy's house for tea, before he takes us home later.

One day, he was meeting us in his car so we could go straight to some out-of-town shops. Alex and I made our way down the road to the usual meeting place when he had the car, our canes moving rhythmically in front of us. All of a sudden one of us hit something with our cane. We went to go around it, but it had moved. Then it happened again—then a third time. Each time we went to go around it, it was gone.

When we got to where my dad was waiting, he couldn't stop laughing. Apparently, we'd been moving a sign down the road. He reckoned it was probably outside a different shop to where it was supposed to be by the time we finished! The thing is, the pavement was so narrow anyway, a sign in the middle of it was sure to be in the way of several people. Funnily enough, we've never met a sign down there since. Perhaps they got the message we'd unintentionally given them!

***

For several months, they had been doing work on a roundabout near where my dad lives. Each time we went around it, he'd give us a progress report. One day, probably somewhere around October, Dad said, "They've got the lights up ready." I was quite enthusiastic as I replied, "Oh! Christmas lights?" He burst out laughing and said he'd meant traffic lights. You can tell how my mind works! If I'd thought about it, there isn't anything much around the roundabout apart from roads, so there wouldn't be Christmas lights. So ever since that day, that roundabout has been known to us all as the "Christmas roundabout".

***

We've discovered a lovely walk in Gloucester along by the canal. The first time I walked along that path with my dad, I said, "I didn't know there was a ten pin bowling alley down here." I was quite surprised that I could hear the balls rolling down the alleys and presumed they must have lots of windows open. Dad hesitated for a moment, then realised what I meant. I was not hearing bowling balls at all, it was the traffic going across the metal bridge over the canal. It really does sound like bowling and shall forever be referred to by us as the bowling ball bridge.

There is also a nice café in a supermarket, where you can sit out on a balcony overlooking the water and being entertained by the pleasure cruise, as it takes its afternoon trip. The commentaries can be quite hilarious! Sometimes we go farther along the canal. It really is quite peaceful. The first time we did that walk, Alex and I were a bit confused when we suddenly turned right—after all, a canal is straight. Dad explained how we had to walk around the basin, where some boats are moored.

As we made that right turn, when we were walking along by the canal a few months later, Alex asked if we were going around the bowl. I was a bit confused, but Dad realised she meant the basin. No prizes for guessing how we refer to that part now!

There was much hilarity one afternoon when we arrived at Dad and Mandy's house. Alex got out of the car through the door behind Dad and followed him to the house, while I came around from the passenger side of the car. I heard the door being unlocked, then opened; then there was a great burst of laughter along with Alex apologising several times! Dad had bent down to pick up the post without telling Alex. Thinking he'd already gone into the house, she stepped up the step and walked straight into the back of him where he was bending down, nearly sending him headfirst into the hallway! He's made sure to tell us when he's picking up the mail ever since!

***

I seem to remember it being a warm sunny afternoon and, after a cup of tea made by Dad, we were off to a shop. Dad had needed to move some things around in the car, so he was out there before us. I must explain here that the back doors of his car slide, so that can sometimes cause confusion in itself when you don't know which way the car is facing. As we were on the drive, Alex knew exactly which way the car was facing. I left her to it and went around the other side and got in. I wondered what Alex was doing, then I heard her sort of grunt before she exclaimed, "It won't piggin' open!" Dad burst out laughing and somehow managed to tell her that the door was already open. He was laughing so much, he had to sit in the car! The open door had looked like a closed back door, next to an open front door. I think it took us all a while to stop laughing after that one!

***

On the main road to Gloucester, they were building a couple of groups of houses. Again, we had the progress report each time we passed. One day Dad said, "I think they've finished those houses there." I asked which ones they were, to which he replied, "The houses for one person." Sounding quite surprised, I said, "They must be small!" He then started laughing and explained that he actually meant they were detached houses and all quite individual. As you can imagine, they are now referred to as the houses for one person.

***

Farther along that road towards home, we occasionally have to stop for the cows to cross, or sometimes there is apparently evidence that they have crossed. One day as we sat waiting for them to be crossed over, we got to talking about how difficult it must be to have part of a farm on each side of a main road. We got to wondering how often they'd have to cross them over, as they were obviously needing to graze on the opposite side to the main farm. Alex said quite innocently, "Perhaps they're crossing over for their tea." The thought of this caused much hilarity, as they were more likely to be crossing over to be milked.

38

I'm the first to admit that my spelling can be hilariously wrong sometimes. There was a time when Gordon, Alan, Alex and I used to sing together, which was a lot of fun. It was during this time when I started to play the baritone ukulele, as Gordon plays guitar and could help me work out the chords. One of the occasions the four of us sang together was for a Sankey evening I'd put together. There was lots of congregational singing, as well as information about Moody and Sankey, together with some songs sung by the four of us.

I'd brailed out the words for Alex and me, putting two pieces of paper in the brailler at once to create a double copy. We were practicing the first week when Alex started laughing. When I asked what I'd done, she said, "You've written the wrong kind of flee! You wrote flea, the itchy kind instead." It didn't surprise me at all. I now remember that the running away kind has two Es, like in feet, as you run with your feet, while the biting kind has ea, like eat!

We had similar confusion when Alex had brailed words for the two of us to sing. She was confused as to whether she should have used "role" or "roll". She thought she'd written the one a ball does and I thought that was the correct one for the context. So whenever we are just singing with no one around, we are likely to sing, "He tells me every care on him to roll, like a ball!" It fits really nicely and just has to be done! I just hope I never sing it in public by mistake!

Sometimes someone sings something so funny that you can't help but laugh—well I can't anyway! The funniest line I've ever heard, and thankfully it was in a practice, was, "O when the Saviour shall make up his bowels!" I'm sure Jewels could look a bit like bowels when written, but that really made us all laugh. I'm afraid it was a while before Alex and I could sing that line again and keep a straight face!

Unfortunately, Alex's wrong word was actually sung during the Sankey evening. Gordon was playing the guitar while I played the ukulele, and I admit that we had got faster as the song went on. We were singing "Down in the valley with my Saviour I will go" which has the chorus, "Follow follow I will follow Jesus". By the time we got to the verse which says, "He will lead me safely in the path that he has trod", Alex was having trouble getting the words in.

I was standing next to her when I wondered if I was hearing right. As I then heard her struggling to keep a straight face and not laugh, I knew I had. Instead of singing "He will lead me safely in the path that he has trod", Alex sang, "He will lead me safely in the f..t that he has trod"! The best bit of all, Jonathan was videoing at the time. It's all there! Alex trying hard not to laugh and me, keeping a straight face for a while, then gradually grinning and trying not to laugh. He said it was like a delayed reaction!

39

Alex and I have known Bruce and Caroline for several years and felt blessed to call them friends, but we thought we'd never have the chance to meet them. However, in the spring of 2019, Caroline came from Canada to visit us. She stayed at my house and we all had such a lovely time together. We began to discover that there are several different words used depending on where you live. The cupboard under the stairs, for example, would be the under-the-stairs closet. The downstairs loo would be a bathroom, although how it could be a bathroom without a bath in it, I'll never know! I love words and all the differences, so we had great fun. Caroline was quite surprised and a little confused when I asked if she would like rocket in her wrap, as she was thinking rocket must actually be the sweet sugary rock we were talking about getting from the seaside. I was, in fact, talking about what she calls arugula, not a bit like the sticks of rock you get at the seaside. I still think rocket is easier to say, though!

***

We tried to do as many typically British things as we could while Caroline was here, including going for a meal at the local pub. It was the middle of the week, so it was quite quiet in there. This changed, however, when we got there with Mum and Chris, as Chris doesn't do anything quietly. The more we tried to get him to talk quieter, the louder he got, especially when he laughed. I don't remember exactly what was said, but Mum said something jokingly about hitting Chris. He only laughed, of course. Caroline had her cane with her. It was a really nice telescopic one and wasn't the usual boring white. We'd all commented on how good it was. A couple of seconds after We'd laughed about Mum hitting Chris, he let out a shout and exclaimed for all to hear, "Ah!!! She got my what's it!" Caroline had picked up her cane and, moving it under the table, had intended to tap Chris on the knee with it. However, she misjudged her aim. He was wearing shorts and the cane had gone right up his shorts leg! That had been the last place Caroline had been aiming for, but it really made us all laugh, especially Chris, who suddenly hoped I wouldn't be getting a cane like Caroline's when I visited her!

*****

It was in August of that same year that I went to visit Bruce and Caroline in Winnipeg. This was the first time I'd flown on my own, and I have to admit it was scary! The thought of getting back off the plane before we took off crossed my mind, but I'm so glad I didn't. I've always had a fear of going places on my own. I can sometimes make myself do it, because I have to, but I'm much happier travelling with someone else. This was not an option, so off I went. What made it even more scary was that I had to get two flights. My constant fear was, what if the first is delayed and I get stranded somewhere I don't know, with people I don't know? I tried to tell myself that wouldn't happen and off I went. However, I didn't go anywhere straightaway, as my first flight kept being delayed. I was thinking constantly of the short space of time between my flights and wondering what would happen. I've experienced delays on trains, and while I don't like the thought of missing a connecting train, I understand the trains enough to know what I have to do to correct the situation. I lost count of the times I checked my watch, as if that was going to change anything. It's not just the travelling alone that's scary, but flying itself. I hadn't flown for ten years previously and I'd forgotten how much I didn't like taking off and landing, as that's the time a plane is most likely to crash, apparently. The idea of being suspended up in midair also seems a bit unnatural to me. To make matters worse, the person I was sat next to didn't speak much English, so I couldn't even have a conversation to try to take my mind off things. The books and music I'd taken didn't help much, either.

I was relieved when the first flight landed, but scared all over again when I realised that, since I'd asked for assistance, I would be the last off the plane. I explained that I had to get another flight, but no one seemed concerned. Finally, I was off the plane, and a very tall man was to take me through Montreal airport. I explained again about the connecting flight to Winnipeg, and he said it should be okay. I have to confess that the word "should" didn't fill me with confidence. He was much taller than I am—most people are—so he had much longer legs. He asked if he was walking too fast, and I insisted he wasn't. I wanted to catch that flight, but several hours of sitting still, along with carrying a bag on my back which I'm not used to, also being so afraid of missing my flight, made it extremely difficult to keep up with him. By the time we'd been through customs and who knows where else, we finally got to the second flight, which I would have missed if it had been on time. This flight was delayed, as they were waiting for fuel. I was so thankful, since it was a real answer to prayer. I hadn't got stranded in an unknown place for who knew how long. By this time I could hear my own heartbeat in my ears and was extremely hot from practically running all the way. I've never been so thankful for a bottle of water as I was then.

I arrived in Winnipeg, where Caroline, Lil, and George were waiting for me. Unfortunately, my case hadn't made it through the airport as quickly as I had and I had to wait until the next day to receive it.

Once I was there, I had a wonderful time. It was so good to spend time with both Bruce and Caroline. We all had some really good conversations, and we even had our own little service one Sunday.

***

I was again fascinated with the different words used. I already knew that a lift was an elevator, but I still get confused as to what a car park is—they call it a parkade. It also confuses me how you enter a building on the first floor, not the ground floor. Here, you go up the stairs to the first floor. I only realised this when I decided to walk all the way down from the twelfth floor, then back up the stairs to get some exercise. I suddenly discovered that I was at the bottom before I thought I would be and wondered at first if I'd miscounted the flights of stairs.

***

On about my second day there, Caroline and I walked to the Dollar store. We had so much fun looking along all the shelves, seeing what they had. Many things we could identify, while others were less obvious. UK readers, please don't stop reading here! We were trying to work out what this one thing was, when Caroline announced, "Oh! It's a fanny pack!" I was horrified and squeaked, "A...what?" I'd never heard that term before. She said it was a bag you wear around your waist and with tears of laughter running down my face, I said, "We call that a bum bag!" Caroline stated, "Well it's the same thing." To which I replied, "It really isn't!"

I then explained that it's the same region, but a different area! Definitely a term not to be used in the UK, although I've since learnt that many people know that the term is used in Canada and the US. I've never laughed so much in a shop before and Caroline was laughing too, once she realised what it meant in the UK. I don't think I could ever bring myself to call it by that name.

***

We did so many lovely things while I was there. One evening, Caroline and I went shopping with Lil. We looked in all sorts of shops, but it was in a clothes shop that the hilarity happened.

I was looking at skirts and dresses when Lil asked, "Do you wear pants?" I managed to keep a straight face as I said, "No, not really." Then I couldn't help but laugh as I explained, "I'm sorry, I knew exactly what you meant, but saying no just sounds so wrong. Back home pants can mean underwear!" The three of us were laughing so much. Lil then tried referring to them as trousers, but I said she should still call them pants!

On the rare occasions that I wear trousers rather than a dress or skirt, I always think of that day and the fun we had.

***

I'm also not sure I ever fully remembered that we were driving on the other side of the road. When we were in the car with Lil and

George, I often forgot which one of them was driving! Seeing Caroline sitting in what I think of as the driver's seat was really funny too! I know Caroline found it strange to sit in what she thought of as the driver's side when she was visiting us here.

***

I managed to return to Canada in March 2020, but was only able to stay a week, as I didn't know if I could get home if I stayed any longer. My best memory of that week was from my last evening. It had been an extremely stressful and disappointing day, but I borrowed Caroline's ukulele and we had a wonderful time of singing together. I hope it won't be too long before I can visit again, I just wish I didn't have to fly!

40

I enjoy exercise, but not the really intense kind! You won't find me at the gym, or running, but I love walking. I feel so much better if I've been moving about, so I bought a Fit bit several years ago, and have tried to get ten thousand steps each day ever since. When I'm in the house, I obviously get some steps, but I often find myself jogging on the spot, or bouncing as it's come to be known, in order to get my steps for the day.

Years ago, long before the Fit bit, I decided to buy a few exercise things to use at home. The one I enjoyed most was a mini trampoline, but it had a problem. You only had to look at it and it squeaked! Not a gentle squeak, but full-on squeaking. It sounded like someone was sawing through rubber! It was quite irritating, and because I was using it in the garage, I imagined everyone hearing this noise and thinking I was strangling cats or something! I got rid of that trampoline and didn't think I'd ever have another, but when I heard about rebounders with bungee cords rather than metal springs, I began to wonder if I might give one a try.

Caroline had told me about these, and, after hearing an audio demonstration of it, I decided I'd get one too. I shopped around and was pleased to find what I was looking for. I placed my order, then waited.

A few days later I had the notification that it had been delivered. I had been out of the house at the time, so I wondered where it had been left. The card which came through my door said that it was in the wheelie bin.

It was a wet evening as I ran outside and around to where the bin is kept. I opened the bin and could feel the box in there. The top of the bin is about my chest height, so when I took hold of the box and tried to pull it upwards, all I ended up doing was tilting the bin towards me on its wheels. When I pulled, the box stayed where it was and the bin came towards me. So I walked backwards, and wedged myself between the bin in front of me and the fence behind me. After a bit of pulling I managed to get the box out.

Relieved, and now dripping with rain, I ran into the house with the box and abandoned it in the hallway, against the radiator. I decided I'd deal with it the next day, as I'd had enough adventures for one night.

Later that evening I went into the...um...little room downstairs. Its door is in the hallway, opposite the radiator. I'm not sure how I managed it, but as I closed the door behind me, I heard a thud in the hallway. Immediately I knew what had happened. Sure enough, somehow I'd managed to hit the box with my elbow and it had fallen behind the door. When I tried to open the door, which opens outwards into the hallway, it would only open a couple of inches. I was stuck in there! I thought about climbing out through the window, but it was too narrow. Thankfully, I had my phone in my pocket, so I didn't panic. If I couldn't get out, I could at least phone Mum for help.

I sat down on the floor and slid my arm out through the small gap. Small wrists can be annoying when you want to buy bracelets, but that day I was truly thankful for them! I slithered my arm around the door and along as far as I could. I was just about able to reach the box with my fingers. I was then thankful for laminate flooring, as I pushed the box as hard as I could with my fingers and it slid along the floor! It slid far enough for me to open the door just enough to squeeze through! I decided I wasn't going to take that chance again, so I moved the box into the kitchen until the next day.

You would think that after all that, my adventures would be over. However, that wasn't so. The following day, I opened up the box and took out the trampoline. Its legs needed to be attached, but before that the bit you bounce on needed to be unfolded. It was folded in four and the first fold was easy to open. I was then left with a semicircular piece which needed to be unfolded to make a circle.

I knew that Caroline had needed help with this part, as it needed the strength of two people to open it out. I think I wondered whether mine might not have such tight bungees or something, so I decided to have a go. I knew I wouldn't have the strength in my arms to open it out, so I inserted my feet between the two halves of the semicircle. I pressed down with my feet and used my arms to push the top half up. I got it so far, but as I tried to push the top half down towards the floor to make a circle, my feet, which were still on the bottom half, lifted up, causing me to go head first over the top! It was at that point that I decided to give up! There was no way I was going to open that on my own.

It did get opened out and the legs attached. I'm now able to enjoy squeak free jogging on the trampoline and so far, it hasn't given me any more adventures!

Conclusion

When I visited Bruce and Caroline in Winnipeg in August 2019, then again in March 2020, I got to visit the church they attend. I was actually there for the last service before the first lockdown and have been watching the services online each Sunday ever since, which has been a real blessing to me. I think Morrow Gospel must be a wonderful church to be a part of, and I really hope I'm able to visit again soon. One of the things they are doing this year is "Pass a Blessing". There are so many ways we can bless one another, giving the gift of something you've made, edible or otherwise, taking the time to make contact with someone, and many more things besides. I hope this book has blessed you and maybe you know someone else who needs a smile and will understand my random humour! If so, pass this book on to them. If it's left sitting on a shelf, it might fall off onto someone's foot or something!